Project Glaive

Bhav Das-Romain

Contents

Dedicated to everyone who needs an escape from expectations.

School Days

My eyes wandered from the classroom door to the long rectangular window on the opposite wall. The last rift anomaly was off the coast of Singapore a few months ago. Another could appear anytime, anywhere. Getting to the proper emergency exit would take too long. It'd be faster to jump onto the overhang under the window, but that was followed by a three story drop. Then again, a long fall was much better than the alternative. But the windows were thick glass and couldn't be opened. Breaking them could prove difficult for most people. Luckily, I had a battering ram in the form of my best friend.

"Ray. Hey," I whispered to get his attention then nodded to the window. "Do you think you could break through that?"

"There'd be glass everywhere, but that wouldn't be an issue," he flexed his right hand to emphasize the point.

It had been a few years since he received a bionic arm in some settlement he never bothered explaining. The guy never wanted for strength, but now he had a defense people could only dream of.

"But getting away from the building could be an issue, depending where the rift is." Ray had a knack for knowing what I was thinking. "We'd probably get separated with everyone scrambling."

It was one of Ray's weaker attempts to brag about his size. Over six feet tall and built like a truck; it was hard *not* to find him in a crowd of high schoolers. Honestly, I was a bit jealous when he shot up in height, but at least I had both my arms. Then again, he had one that could literally punch through a wall so maybe it wasn't much of a handicap.

"I really don't think that'd be an issue," I said.

"Anand, Ray, what's your homework for the week?" Mrs. Oakley asked loudly.

Her stern eyes glared at us from behind thick horn rimmed glasses. Seeing hers awkwardly resting on the bridge of her nose made me nervously fix my own. Ray looked to me for a hint, but I was just as lost and couldn't hide the embarrassment from my face. A familiar grumble sounded from our teacher. It was often aimed at us which made it all the more embarrassing.

"The worksheet coming towards you is due on Friday. Class is almost over. I'm sure you can save your conversation till then."

"Sorry," I replied involuntarily.

"We'll work on it, Mrs. Oakley," Ray said.

It felt like the whole room was laughing at us, but Ray was unphased. I had trouble concentrating on whatever else Mrs. Oakley said until the end of class. Only once other kids started packing their bags did I feel like I could focus again. Papers rustled loudly which in turn made students' volume rise as they talked about their plans for the evening. I carefully put my papers in the designated folder before slotting it into my backpack followed by my laptop. Ray simply scrunched everything into his. Somehow he'd find it later, but I'd given up on understanding his storage system a long time ago.

The loud banging of shut lockers mixed with cascading voices all throughout the bustling halls. Ray stood in front of me to carve a path through the crowd towards the stairs. There was only a single wing of Middleton High School that went up to the third floor and unfortunately our day ended up here. While both stairwells led to an exit, one would put us behind the school another crowded area. The one we preferred, though slower, got us to the side of the building.

The intense scent of flora was the first thing I noticed after school everyday. Flowers burst through the last remnants of snow littering the ground. Mud squelched underfoot as we cut corners to parking lots near local businesses. The library was, for all intents and purposes, a straight shot from the school. At least five minutes got cut from the walk over when using our shortcut. Ray was always concerned about which path to take in hopes of getting to our meeting spot first. Keeping up with his natural stride was a workout I'd grown accustomed to over the years. Sometimes it felt like he deliberately sped up so I wouldn't have the chance to walk leisurely. Then again, he may not have thought about it at all since he was focused on a different competition.

Ray barreled through the front doors and beelined for our destination, but I slowed down to greet the librarians. A lineup of newly released books were displayed on an acrylic shelf a few steps from the entrance past the security gates. The ever-present stench of printed press wafted through the building. The familiar rows of books were being perused by the same people who dropped by after school everyday. None were who I was looking for. They all sat at a table in the corner of the lounging area. Ray was arguing with two girls whose things were already set on our usual table. Eve, a girl with dark skin and bouncy locs, flashed a toothy grin at me before turning back to Ray. Next to her was Sarah, fixing the statically charged hair that clung to her headphones.

"You're gonna have to try way harder to get a win," Eve said in a voice dripping with condescension.

"Yeah, that zero in your win column's getting dusty." Sarah added.

"Oh, shut up. Your classes get out before ours," Ray complained as he slumped into a spot next to Eve.

I took the last spot at the table. "You could always opt out of the race. It's stacked against you."

"Look, one day, someone's gonna let us out early and I'll swoop in here before Eve. Then, I'll drop out of the race."

"What if I quit before that?" Eve asked with a smirk.

"That won't happen. You like beating me too much." Ray flashed his signature wide smile.

Eve tilted her head in thought. "That... is very true."

Ray grabbed a comic out of his backpack and settled in. Eve returned to taking notes while Sarah turned her focus back to her laptop. She kept one headphone off while working near us. I didn't bother starting on my homework to avoid a headache later. Instead, I pulled out my laptop and opened the Rift Report website; a forum discussing rift appearances ever since the first one over two decades ago. The original creator had yet to post misinformation regarding anything rift related. Aside from the rift follow ups, most articles were posted at irregular intervals. It was likely to avoid detection.

Every theory about rifts only piqued my curiosity further. Revisiting them had become a daily habit. Information died down between anomalies, but there was always the chance that something new was discovered. Hours of classes made it possible that I might miss updates. But there was a very real threat to my safety if I didn't keep up in my classes. Much more so than a theoretical rift appearance.

While everyone knew something came out of the portals, no one knew what. At least no one outside of the Global Protection Agency. They absolutely had a hand in getting rid of any proof citizens had amassed of Riftwalkers. The only picture I ever saw was blurry and impossible to analyze. I'd saved it and backed it up in a bunch of places, but the files all vanished. Even so, I remembered every little detail of the photo. Some sort of animalistic humanoid was moving across a city street. Based on the quality of the photo it was either extremely fast or the photographer was unskilled. I dreaded the former being true.

Unfortunately, there didn't seem to be any new info today. At least none I could find before my hour was up. The familiar alarm on my phone grabbed everyone's attention.

"I still can't believe you have to go home early this week," Ray grumbled.

"Family time has to be equal if I'm spending the weekend with my friends," I recited.

"Don't do that shit with me, Anand."

"Lay off, Ray. You know how Arjun is," Eve interjected.

Ray huffed. "Sure, but Anand doesn't need to be like him."

"He's not," Sarah said sharply. She patted my shoulder gently and smiled. "You're fine. Text us when you get home."

"See y'all later," I murmured while quickly stowing my things before leaving the table.

My friends' kindness did little to diminish the humiliation I felt every time I left like this. Them knowing what my parents were like didn't make it any easier to deal with. Splitting off from my group made the walk home lonelier even if people intermittently greeted me. Every step towards the house, a familiar weight in my stomach grew. I appreciated it as much as I hated it. It put me in the right mindset of an obedient son. One who didn't talk back or laugh. One who didn't share his interests or personal research. They'd overheard it before when my friends visited, but I nipped that in the bud after a few arguments.

Mom and Dad only cared about how my interests hindered their goals for me. If something got in the way of the path they set out, it should be removed with haste. Luckily, if I never brought it up, they ignored it. The emptiness I forced upon myself put me in a perpetual state of anger, but I did my best to keep it contained. There was no place for reactive emotion in their house. Not for me, at least. I could get through it. I'd been doing it my whole life. What helped was having a place where I could breathe.

Stepping up to the front door of my parents' house always felt daunting. Logically, the bushes of flowers around the perimeter should be beautiful. The tan facade was positively domestic and simple decorations that hung year-round welcomed anyone who approached. But I only felt the overwhelming pressure of the people inside. The click of the key was a bell that alerted them of my presence. Nothing could beat the constant scent of curry wafting through the halls. I quickly removed my shoes and stowed them before walking from the foyer to the kitchen. The rough carpet turned to smooth tile that was cold to the touch. Mom toiled over a large pot filled with sizzling meat and spices. Her long black hair was tied into a tight ponytail, but some strands still stuck to her sweaty brow.

"How was your day, *beta*?" she asked with a soft smile.

"Good, normal."

"And your friends?"

"They're fine. We'll hang out this weekend."

I leaned on the kitchen counter. Mom knew I wasn't saying everything, but she couldn't complain since it was her own tactic. But I also got my curiosity from her and she couldn't hide the frustrated look from her face. I was stupid for not giving her all the information she wanted.

"I told them I had to get home for chores," I lied.

Mom nodded. "Okay. Get the table set and call Dad up."

I didn't mind the bit where I needed to set the table. Calling up my father was the task I'd rather avoid. A chill ran down my spine as I approached the basement door. Going downstairs to his office would be moronic. Then he could berate me without Mom around. It's not like she took my side or anything, but she could at least get him to ease up. No, the better option was to scream for my father to call him upstairs.

"DAD, DINNER'S READY!"

I didn't bother waiting for him to start eating. On the other hand, Mom didn't even serve herself until my father had eaten his first bite. It took him almost ten minutes to finally come to the table. Even while standing a head shorter than me, the intimidating aura radiating off my father made me feel like a child. There wasn't any hair on the man's head which made his permanent glare of disappointment all the more prominent. I nervously ran a hand through my wavy hair then fixed my glasses.

"Hello, Anand. How was school? Do you have any homework?" Dad asked with an icy voice. He believed it sounded stoic, but it just made me feel small.

"Yes." I noticed myself slouching and quickly sat up straight, but never took my eyes off my plate. "A few assignments due by the end of the week. I'm... working on a report about rift anomalies."

A low grunt made his disappointment clear. I chanced a look and saw his familiar frown.

"What class is that for?" he grumbled.

"Interplanetary Analysis. It's one of my electives," I replied meekly, bracing for his onslaught of complaints.

"Remember to focus on your proper classes. You're not even the top of your class and you waste time on hobbies. You can't be successful that way!" Within seconds he was on the brink of screaming.

I tried not to look sullen. "Sorry."

"The food is getting cold," Mom said.

Dad grunted then slowly took a first bite. As if on command, Mom began serving herself.

"I have more work tonight," Dad said. "Try not to waste all your time goofing off on your game. You know I never agreed to you having that. I will sell it if you keep getting distracted. Finish your work and try to get ahead."

I nodded. "Right."

The second there was no food on my plate I took it to the sink then escaped to my room. It was a blessing that I wasn't expected to ask to be excused. Whenever I walked across the carpeted floor it felt like pin pricks against the soles of my feet. Only in the little room where I kept my things did I feel comfortable. The bed centered on the far wall was a hand-me-down queen covered in a thick sherpa blanket. My closet was filled with graphic tees and button-downs plus a handful of kurtas for special occasions. My usual spot was a desk in the corner covered in knickknacks and surrounded by posters.

It was a single space in my parent's house where I could lie to myself; believe that it was possible to get off the path Dad set out. Joining the GPA was a distant dream, but broaching the subject was nerve-wracking. The very thought caused me to spiral. I had to make an active effort to calm down. It took about fifteen minutes for my quickened heartbeats to slow. I couldn't scream or cry or be a bother while trying to maintain an even keel. Suffocating was a better alternative. Hell, maybe dying was. But then I wouldn't see my friends. The thought of that was worse than dealing with my father.

Silently, I began working through the day's assignments. Nothing was overly difficult. In fact, I could probably finish them before coming home. But when I used to do that I'd get berated for not doing enough. Or that I was lying about completing my homework so I could waste time playing games. I ended up doing some assignments twice just to prove I knew how to do the work. All of the accusations of laziness could be disproven if Dad checked my records, but challenging him was idiotic.

Even distracted, it didn't take long to get through my home-work. A familiar tune rang from my phone and a notification sat on the lock screen indicating a message on the group chat.

did u die -Ray

No. Sorry, forgot to ping y'all -Anand

all gud -Ray

We have trig homework -Sarah

Is that a question or a statement? -Eve

Question -Sarah

There's a couple problems to solve, yeah. -Eve

The conversation quickly devolved from there. Maybe the intermittent chatting was what caused my grades to be below my potential. Dad had said something similar once. But my assignments got done and consistently received As and Bs. He was probably wrong about my potential. But telling Dad that was a literal death sentence. Not the part that I wasn't as smart as expected; rather that he was wrong about anything ever. The thought of it made me chuckle, but I quickly stifled it. Expressing joy was "welcome" in the house, but if it happened when I wasn't playing a game I'd be questioned. And I wouldn't have an answer my parents liked.

I quickly finished up the rest of my assignments then booted up my PlayStation. It was a gift I'd received after months of begging. Mom might stand on the sidelines during my father's tirades, but she was usually the best parent I could ask for. With an unfortunate amount of effort, I stopped worrying about them and turned my attention to the console. Killing time with it was better than wallowing for hours before bed.

Emergency

Every morning followed the same routine of a quick shower, breakfast, and then waiting for Dad to be ready to drop me off. When he was, I hopped into the passenger seat of his sedan and readied myself for whatever he wanted to complain about during the short drive. For once the topic was something of interest: the GPA. Mainly because their presence was suddenly felt throughout Middleton. Most cities had a single GPA base, but they never patrolled like they were now. They prowled the streets armed with a myriad of weapons and clad in sectioned gray body armor yet no one feared them. "Only the best humanity has to offer" could pass the extensive testing and training required to get in, at least according to GPA Director Jillian Graves.

Forced detours took us to main roads we normally avoided. Long drives with my father were a nightmare, but it was nice to see GPA vehicles in action. Modified motorbikes and armored jeeps idled near large intersections surrounding massive carriers known as Runners. I hadn't seen train-like vehicles since an elementary school field trip. They were just as magnificent as

I remembered. A distinct logo was engraved on every agent and tool; three four pointed stars housing the letters "GPA." Even Dad's incessant griping about slow traffic couldn't ruin my wonderment.

The school perimeter had half a dozen agents roaming nearby as well. Some chatted with teachers and students while others simply kept watch. Once I got out of the car I wanted to join the conversation, but if Dad caught me talking to the GPA he'd never let me hear the end of it. I wasn't ready for that yet. Instead I rushed into the school and headed for my locker. Thanks to the block schedule I didn't actually have class for almost two hours.

"How far'd you get last night?" Ray asked from the other side of my locker door.

"Unlocked a few new weapons and combos. But I'm—"

"Probably gonna stick to punching. Yeah, yeah. You really should try some of the other weapons. There's two different ones called glaives, but I think it's a typo."

"Didn't you once tell me there's been a lot of stuff called glaives throughout history?" I asked while shutting my locker. "Might not be a typo. Different question: Why are you wearing your aviators inside?"

Ray shrugged. "I thought I'd need them today."

"Sure, it's kinda bright outside. Still doesn't explain why they're still on."

"You wear sunglasses inside all the time."

"Transition lenses taking time to change is different than wearing a normal pair of sunglasses indoors."

"Is it really, though?"

"Yes! What are— Nope, not worth it." I threw my hands up in surrender. "Where's Eve?"

"Headed to class already. Had some questions for her teacher. Not gonna ask about Sarah?" Ray grinned slyly and slapped my back as we walked through the hall.

"I hate you," I grumbled. "And no. She probably got caught in traffic with the GPA around. Any ideas why they're so active today?"

"You're the guy I'd normally ask."

"Good point. I'll look into it and let you know what I find."

"Sick."

Ray swung his left hand towards me and I slapped it with mine. He headed for the second floor while I made my way to the school library. Sarah would know where to find me. Most people went to the cafeteria during their open block, but the wireless connection wasn't as strong there. That left few students in the library, making it the perfect place for me to discretely research the GPA and possible rift a. My parents already gave me weird looks because of my interest in rifts; I didn't need others to as well.

Normally it would take me getting to the usual forums to find any new information. Instead, the local news feed I had sitting on my desktop already had reports about the GPA. Apparently they'd begun mobilizing a few hours ago around 5 AM. How they did so quietly likely had something to do with their proprietary technology. I immediately tried to send a message to my friends, but couldn't. The message was accepted by the system, but refused to be sent to the others. I paid it no mind since that happened at school sometimes.

Looking further into the GPA presence revealed they had planted Runners throughout the city as if preparing for something. It didn't sit right in my gut. I searched for any historical records of similar GPA outings across the world. There wasn't any readily found information, but the Rift Report's peculiar posting pattern left remnants that painted a clearer picture. The GPA was on guard in Singapore months ago. Sicily before that. I quickly texted the group without checking if the message sent. There was more research to be done. Unfortunately, pages began stuttering. I tried exiting and loading a new one, but I only got artifacts of previously loaded sites. Other students started grumbling about the network followed by the staff. I wanted to check if my friends were experiencing it too, but before I could an alarm blared throughout the building. The ear piercing tone rang through my body and put everyone on alert. After several tones a message played.

This is an emergency announcement. A rift anomaly has appeared in the proximity of your location. Remain calm. Please follow emergency evacuation instructions to move to a safe lo-

cation. Do not deviate from GPA instructions. This is not a drill. I repeat...

Fear was plastered on everyone's faces as they scrambled for the doors. The halls were already packed with people pushing their way towards the exits. Every year students were informed of where to go in the case of a rift related emergency. My best options were the main doors to the south of the building or the Performing Arts Center to the east. While it wasn't easier, fewer people were moving eastward so I opted for that. Unfortunately, the crowd stopped short in the hall. Ceiling high windows surrounded the entrance to the auditorium and made it impossible to miss what was happening outside.

Cloudy darkness had taken the place of clear skies and a bright sun. Blades of purple light cut through the sky and expanded into jagged portals of swirling ink. They hovered unnaturally while creating pocketed disasters. Fire rained out of one while a torrent of water gushed from another. Lightning storms ripped apart normal vehicles while alien stones destroyed anything they touched. There were some spectacles I couldn't even describe. Only GPA vehicles could handle the frightening onslaught. Within the thunderous sounds of nature, I started hearing bestial roars and horrified screams.

Agents outside equipped what appeared to be firearms and aimed at the closest rifts. Instead of bullets they fired out a shining beam of light that tethered to the portals and began stitching them closed. I knew stitchers were a crucial tool in the GPA arsenal but had never seen them in person. They were fascinating but incredibly slow.

"Move!" I yelled and pushed through the crowd to the Runner. "We gotta go now!"

It didn't matter that some people thought I was rude. They snapped out of their shock and began moving for the exit. GPA agents and teachers guided the students through a temporary tunnel that had been installed this morning. I couldn't process how something so sturdy was made so quickly, but now wasn't the time for that. Since I'd been at the front of the crowd I was on the first idling Runner. The massive transport felt a lot more cramped with all 180 passengers. Drivers sat in a separated area which held the only window to the outside world. The passenger section was a large block of metal that kept everyone safe within its barren walls. As the transport began to move, a loud hum echoed through the vehicle. It wasn't enough to block out the sounds of destruction outside, but it dulled them.

Looking around the crowd, I quickly spotted Ray. There was too much fearful chatter for me to feel comfortable shouting for him. Instead, I shimmied over slowly. Only then did I realize Eve was with him. Their morning classes being close explained how they ended up together.

"I'm guessing the GPA knew this was coming," Eve said while nervously fiddling with her choker.

I nodded. "Somehow, yeah. Rift Report said it's the norm. I never caught it before."

"It's not something you'd usually look for."

"How long's it been since we started moving?" Ray asked.

"Couple of minutes," Eve answered. "We're heading to the bunker under the Marriott so it'll still be a bit."

Ray huffed. "I hate this!"

It was rare to see Ray actually mad about something. Sure he might act like it when we rag on him, but seeing him get frustrated was concerning. It also didn't really make sense. He'd had first hand experience with rift related activity before. Waiting around and being useless was part of being a civilian. It's why our group wanted to join the GPA and make a difference. I rested a hand on his shoulder and silently expressed he had my support as well as Eve's.

There was still no sign of Sarah and it was starting to nag at me. Checking my phone, I noticed no messages I'd sent today had actually gone to the others. That was until the Runner came to a stop. Slowly, the back wall fell outward to act as a ramp and simultaneously our group chat was updated. All my messages went through as well as a few random ones from this morning. Any semblance of relief I had vanished as I read Sarah's last message.

"She's trapped," I muttered.

Ray forcibly turned my hand to read the message before passing the phone to Eve. People poured out of the Runner towards an opening built into the side of the nearby hotel. It was a large ramp that went into an underground bunker. Runners were lined up alongside it with the massive crowd slowly moving inside. I walked along the edge absentmindedly, looking towards the road we'd come from.

"She says she's at Room and Board." Eve informed us.

Sarah loved stopping by the local boardgame store to look at cards on free block days. That should've never been a threatening prospect. With how much time had passed, and the fact she was still there, it felt unlikely she'd get GPA assistance. I stood at the edge of the crowd, only a few steps from the last Runner in the convoy. From here it was possible to see hundreds of rifts raining hell across the city. Sealing them was taking all the agents' attention. Others were distracted by panicked questions from civilians.

I grabbed my phone from Eve and she pulled out her own. We'd all shared our locations in case of emergencies. Since phone lines were working again it was possible to see Sarah's lone icon a couple miles away from us. There was nothing I could think to do, but stare. Yet my body wouldn't move towards the bunker.

"Something's there with her," Eve informed us with a cold, fearful voice.

Ray let out a slow, shaky breath. "A Riftwalker."

The word scarcely left his mouth before I'd broken into a full sprint out of the crowd. I was halfway down the block when a Runner honked its ear piercing horn to grab my attention. An agent quickly exited to give chase. All the working out I'd done was nothing compared to how the GPA trained. The man surged towards me and no matter how much I pushed myself, it felt pointless. I could feel the encroaching grasp of the agent on my collar.

Suddenly, I was thrown forward by an explosive blast behind me. The agent was thrown to the side by whatever force came from the rift overhead.

Ray pulled me up and slapped my back. "Lead the way."

My footing was barely secure before I dashed off again.

"This is insane!" Eve shouted, only a few steps behind.

"Just get to Sarah! We'll figure it out later," I instructed. "Just don't do anything stupid."

Ray laughed heartily. "We're long past that."

Rescue

Air sizzled like a live wire across the city. Cascading rifts let off a purple glow that tainted everything in sight. Some had been stitched closed and vanished, but several dozen still assaulted the land. Abandoned vehicles littered the roads, some beeping incessantly. GPA agents moved in groups as they fought back unseen threats. I would have loved to catch a glimpse of a Riftwalker, but doing so would get us caught before we helped Sarah. Years of navigating our suburb made it easy to sneak past GPA groups. Every alley was a welcome route yet all of us hesitated in case a monster appeared from the shadows. Each passing moment made the nagging voice in my head grow louder. It was my father berating me for acting foolishly on impulse.

"Focus, Anand," Eve said, pushing me out from the corner we hid behind. "We're almost there."

I nodded and continued towards the small strip mall that housed Room and Board. The parking lot would normally be empty at this time, but now had numerous cars throughout with no regard to the painted spots. The two story Willy

Street Co-op at the end of the mall looked more decrepit than I'd ever seen it. All the smaller stores had lost their homely charm and taken on a haunting quality. Lights flickered dimly past shattered windows. Shelves crumpled onto the goods they once held. Trickles of blood and fluorescent orange ooze traced shards of glass. The shining liquids were splattered across multiple surfaces.

"Sarah!" Ray yelled towards the seemingly empty mall.

I smacked him lightly on the back of the head. "Shut up! We need to be careful. Set up your earbuds."

Ray fished a pair out of his pocket and asked, "Why?"

"Communication," Eve answered before I could. "Get on VC."

"Right. Be careful and don't do anything rash… again." Ray fiddled with his single earbud then whispered, "Can you hear me?"

"Loud and clear," I replied as we separated. "I'll head to Room and Board."

Ray went towards Willy Street Co-op while Eve went to the pet store at the other end of the mall. Whispered calls for Sarah intermittently came through the comms. Eve and I sounded cautious, but Ray was surprisingly nonchalant. If I didn't know any better I'd call it stupidity. But Ray's ability to stay calm in dire situations was one of his best traits. A skill he'd trained consciously when his dad was around. Honestly, it made sense Eve was so scared since she had lost her parents more recently. I couldn't help, but regret sending her off alone, but it was our only choice. We needed to find Sarah quickly and regroup then find a GPA convoy.

Creeping through the damaged store, I focused on the sounds around me. Rift anomalies wrecking the city made it harder to discern between destruction and footsteps. Whether they were a Riftwalker or Sarah didn't matter as long as I got more information about our situation. That belief lasted until I came across the bodies.

It looked like three people, but it was hard to deduce how many had been sliced into ribbons. There was too much damage to organs to figure out what I was looking at. A deep pool of blood spread across the ground, seeping into the carpet. Tears flowed freely as my body boiled. I couldn't stop myself from vomiting. The only source of comfort was that I couldn't recognize any remnants as Sarah. Once I could move without heaving, I ran to the back of the store.

Sweat dripped from my brow as I wandered the damaged play area. We'd spent our fair share of time goofing off here and seeing it destroyed was heartbreaking. I couldn't figure out how some of it occurred since the rifts were outside, but I had a strong hunch. Quickening my search, I ended up in the storage room where boardgames to borrow filled the shelves. The familiar sight of a girl examining the games sent a wave of relief through me. My racing heart went from fearful to hopeful.

I called out to her as I approached. "Sarah?"

Long scrapes ran along her arms and legs from running through the store. She looked to be shaking and I prepared to ease her concerns. I stopped short when Ray yelled through the voice chat.

"Found Sarah! Leaving Willy Street Co-op."

A chill ran down my spine as I got within arm's reach of the girl in front of me. What turned to face me was a grotesque *creature*. The cuts on its form were, in actuality, large cavities where muscles should be. Mutated flesh took the appearance of clothing while its "body" was a dehydrated husk. Instead of eyes it had cavernous black pits with small white dots that looked like full moons in the vastness of space. An involuntary whimper escaped my throat as the creature gurgled out incomprehensible noises. I backed away with shaky steps.

The monster tilted its head, letting out a raspy sigh as it followed. Grasping blindly behind myself, I found nothing to use as a weapon, but I didn't dare take my eyes off the monster to get a better look. Unfortunately, I missed my footing and tripped over some fallen debris. The creature sauntered towards me and knelt down. Its face started to melt while bones bent and broke. A cackle crept out of its misshapen maw; amused by its bodily transformation. It was impossible not to recognize the new form as a twisted reflection of myself.

With its long nails outstretched, the monster lifted my glasses and cut my cheek in the process. Orange ooze dripped from a wound on its wrist into my cut while it awkwardly donned the spectacles. It recoiled in disgust and threw them aside, shattering them against rubble. Even with the horror bearing down on me I heard the voice of my father complaining about me breaking my glasses.

"Anand! Roll right!" Eve yelled.

I didn't have the luxury to figure out where it came from and just followed the order. If I hadn't I would've been crushed by the shelf that toppled onto my assailant. The creature stirred under the planks as Eve grabbed my arm and pulled me to my feet. Both of us kept our eyes off the destroyed bodies in the front half of the store.

"Run!" I shouted.

"Come to Willy's storage. We need to hide," Ray commanded.

"We need to get to the GPA."

"There's no agents nearby," Eve said. "This is the best option for now."

I clicked my tongue. "Shit. Okay."

As we leapt out of the window I heard the shelf shatter behind us. The monster's glare was almost a physical force. No matter how fast we ran it felt only inches away. For some reason, Ray was waiting outside like an immovable wall. With a mighty roar he attempted to attack. It quickly turned into a scream of pain after he made contact. Before getting launched backwards, the monster dug its claws into Ray's bionic arm and used the momentum to rip it apart. I only stopped long enough to grab him and drag him away.

"Why is it always my arm?!" he complained while leading us to Sarah's hiding spot.

Rows upon rows of large metal shelves lined with various goods occupied the storage room. It wasn't a full warehouse, but there was plenty of space to maneuver and hide. Some products had clattered to the floor, turning into a makeshift obstacle course. With the opportunity to breathe, we all reconvened between a small group of filled pallets.

Seeing Sarah made me feel like an idiot for mistaking the monster for her. There weren't just a couple scrapes on her arms. Shredded pieces of clothing hung limply under the weight of bloody cuts. The flowing hair she took so much pride in was slick with streaks of red and glowing orange. Tears were slowly drying as she calmed her nerves.

Without thinking I hugged her. "I'm glad you're okay."

"Those people survive?" she asked softly while hugging me back. "They saved me from the Riftwalker."

Trying to explain made me gag so I just shook my head.

"We're not in the clear yet," Ray said.

I expected him to ask me for a plan like usual, but instead he was looking towards Eve. Even with my blurry vision I could tell she was in pretty bad shape. She kept wringing her choker and muttering to herself. Her bones must have been clattering from how much she shook. I'd never have guessed she could lose her composure so completely.

Slowly, she looked at Ray and gulped hard. "I can't do it."

"You have to, Eve. I'm down an arm," Ray replied with a surprising amount of calm for someone with a recently missing limb. "Even if they're prototypes—"

"We don't even know if they'll work! Otherwise you would've used it earlier."

"I tried! I mistimed it."

"You didn't need to time it!"

"I didn't want to freak anyone out."

Eve threw up her hands. "Oh my god! You were trying to make an entrance! NOW?!"

The sound of loud scraping echoed through the corridor. For some reason Eve and Ray kept arguing even with impending danger so close. Neither were normally this stubborn. Though these circumstances were anything, but normal. No amount of studying or theorizing could have prepared us for facing a Riftwalker. Ray and Eve had clearly planned something, but it had fallen apart. Something idiotic happening to Ray wasn't new, but Eve had only been this scared once before.

"Shit. Ray, leave it!" I commanded once the realization dawned on me. "That thing is coming this way. Either we need to run or you need to let me in on this plan. The three of you are worse off than me."

Ray huffed and clenched his teeth. Slowly, he peered over the edge of a pallet to look for an exit. After a brief scan, he crouched back down and handed me his aviators.

"It's coming from the only route out of here," he said. "Plan B, it is."

He nodded to me and I cautiously put on the aviators. While the tint was present it didn't worsen my eyesight like expected.

Honestly, they were better at correcting my vision than my prescription lenses.

"What the hell?" I asked.

"You just offered to be in on the plan." Ray griped.

"Not that. I can see better with these."

Ray furrowed his brow and muttered. "Gotta make note of that. Actually, that's great news. It'll make it easier to fight."

"What are you talking about?" I asked.

"Being a superhero!" Ray was positively beaming.

I clenched my fists. "That doesn't explain anything!"

"Sure it does," Ray argued then realized I was right. "I'll explain."

The Riftwalker had foregone stealth and was angrily storming through the storage room. Pallets were flipping through the air, spraying goods in every direction. Footsteps marched rapidly toward us.

"The code word is unsheathe. It won't work on its own, though. You need to visualize a transformation," Ray explained. "It's just a prototype, it should be fine against most attacks." He paused briefly then said, "On second thought, try not to get hit. What matters is that you can fight back."

He seemed to be done talking so I asked, "Then what?"

"Huh?"

"What do I do after fighting? Doesn't the plan have a goal?"

"Getting to safety." Sarah said then turned to the others. "You don't expect Anand to kill it, do you?"

Eve shook her head. "No, we hit this wall too. It's why Ray doesn't have a real backup plan. Anand, force it through a rift. Shouldn't be an issue if you can overpower it."

Wooden boards shattered as a whole metal shelf was toppled and its contents went everywhere. The Riftwalker roared in frustration. I rose to my feet to get a good look at it. Its form was no longer human. Its bony skeleton stretched to seven feet with long skinny arms and legs. Slender claws extended from each finger that effortlessly lifted anything blocking its path.

"Wendigo," I said without thinking.

Slowly, the creature turned to face me and a smile sliced across its face. My mind blanked as it began running towards me. The others stood up behind me in shock. I felt them shaking me, but I only focused on the monster. I wasn't scared. Maybe that's what surprised me.

I was awestruck by a mythological form I'd read about. Confusion about Ray's unknown plan weighed on me. Hell, I even felt happy to sacrifice myself for my friends. The fear in the pit of my stomach was negligible. While the others began to scramble over the boxes behind me, I stood my ground. I heard Sarah call out to me, but Eve pulled her away.

Wendigo's claws sliced through a steel beam to bring a metal shelf down before throwing it at me. Some strange part of me found its unnatural strength fascinating.

"Anand, focus!" Ray roared. "Unsheathe! Fight!"

"Right."

I slid my right foot back to angle myself at forty-five degrees while still facing the oncoming threat. Never before had I been thankful for my parents forcing me into extracurricular boxing as a kid. Right now I was more annoyed they'd pulled me out a few years ago. But I could complain about that later. The large projectile was rapidly approaching. With my fists raised just below my eyes, I steadied my breath.

"Unsheathe."

The sunglasses shattered into a shining metal liquid that engulfed my body in a flash. I thought I'd suffocate, but was instead wrapped in a warm embrace. My clothing fused into a tight carbon fiber full-body suit. A blue and white chest-piece covered the upper torso with armor plating lining the arms. More pieces appeared across the suit's legs, gloves, and boots. The helmet was relatively plain with extra plating near my jaws. Most noticeably, the visor was a chunk ripped out of the front in the shape of a "v" that extended off the sides. Thankfully, it maintained vision correction.

I didn't feel like myself. Seeing the interface inside was an out of body experience. Information about the suit and surroundings masked any sense of self. There was no meek failure of a son or suicidal martyr facing a monster. There was only the armored warrior.

Unsheathed

The cobalt warrior threw his hands forward faster than the boy in the suit ever could. They slammed into the shelf and it bent around the point of contact before clattering to the floor. There wasn't the slightest twinge of pain.

A modulated voice came from the suit. "What is this?"

"I call it Gale!" Ray yelled from behind.

Examining it wasn't an option as Wendigo continued approaching. Gale stood his ground and took a fighting stance. He easily ducked under the monster's massive claw swipe. Several punches flew out and all landed with a swift impact that pushed the creature back. Instead of waiting for it to react, Gale surged forward. Powerful jabs drilled into its bony chest. Orange ichor poured out of cuts in its sickly grey hide.

A powerful blade struck Gale's side and flung him away. While it hurt to get hit, the attack didn't break through the armor. He landed awkwardly on his feet then rushed back towards the Riftwalker. It held its claws in front of it like a wall. Without stopping, Gale lunged forward and forced his fist through the latticed blades. Wendigo screamed in pain, but it remained standing. The strike should have sent it flying, but only broke past its defense. Luckily, it also caused the Riftwalker to completely forget about Ray, Eve, and Sarah. The monster's hunt only had one target. Gale rushed into its reach, but made no attempt to attack. Instead, he weaved around its long legs and ran for the exit. The others took the chance to escape from a different exit.

Given that Gale was able to fight evenly with a Riftwalker, it should be possible to send it through a rift. Many in the area had closed and the presence of the GPA had diminished. A small group of agents nearby were still working on a halfway stitched rift at ground level. They all looked at Gale with confusion as he approached. That quickly turned to fear upon seeing the eight foot tall Riftwalker chasing him. One continued using her stitcher on the rift while her five teammates drew assault weapons.

"Hold!" Gale yelled. "I need the rift!"

He wasn't sure why, but the GPA agents took pause. They looked between each other, quickly discussed something, then stepped behind their jeep for protection. The layered panels on the side of the vehicle made the perfect path. There was no doubt that the loud monster was still giving chase. When Gale reached the jeep, he planted a foot against the side before running upwards. At the top he leapt off, flipped and sailed over the Riftwalker to land behind it. It might be able to run quickly, but had proven slow when turning.

There was a brief moment when it tried to pivot and lost its balance. It was the perfect opening for Gale to tackle the monster into the rift. The stitchers beam burned a line across the monster's face as it crossed into the portal. Closing the rift must have been further along than Gale realized since it vanished near instantly.

He backed away quickly while the agents examined the empty space, getting away before they could interrogate him. More important questions were piling up in Gale's mind. It would take an unprecedented amount of time and resources to make a suit like this. There was no telling what allowed it to magically appear with a single word. Why the body inside could suddenly operate beyond peak capacity had to be explained. Thankfully, it seemed those with answers were two of his closest companions: Ray Kekoa and Eve Stetson.

Father's Legacy

We snuck back into the bunker with obvious scrapes and bruises. Most people just gave us pity for having been left behind during evacuation. Apparently we weren't the only ones which wasn't all that unusual based on my years of research. Rifts were so aggressive that the GPA had to focus primarily on stitching once Runners made their escape. That resulted in a blindspot when it came to saving evacuees who got missed.

The next few days were a blur. School was closed for the rest of the week while Madison and Middleton went through repairs. Apparently the rift anomalies had done more damage than the infrastructure could handle. All the extra construction went relatively unnoticed.

Classes were online, but I barely paid attention. I could barely see without my glasses and there were other things to worry about. Ray and Eve adamantly avoided the topic of the armor. Privacy was at the forefront of their minds. The earliest I could learn more was over our weekend hangout. Until then, I couldn't avoid the consequences of our escapade like the others.

Mom and Dad wouldn't let me out of their sight except for class until repairs were completed. Some of the caution came from concern, at least in the case of Mom. My father's punishment stemmed from what he perceived as a failing on my part.

"You act like you know so much, but could not even evacuate properly!" he yelled. "You got hurt and for what? To show off that you could get to a bunker alone?"

That was the dumbest suggestion I'd ever heard. I wouldn't have run off if not to help my friend, but that wasn't something he needed to know. With Arjun, silence was always the best option.

"Do you know how much your glasses cost? You can't just let them break," Dad insisted. "Now I'll have to take a day off and pull you from class for an appointment. Do you see the trouble you cause?"

"We were in danger. Ray lost his arm," I said meekly. "I didn't think—"

"You never do! *I* have to pay for your glasses. Ray's family has other means."

"If me paying for my glasses will make you stop, I can do that." I regretted the words as soon as they left my mouth.

Dad's eyes went wide and his nostrils flared. "What was that?"

Now that I'd spoken up, I couldn't stop myself. "Everyone was in a bad spot and sacrificing my glasses didn't seem like an issue. You're right, I shouldn't make that decision if I don't pay for them. So I will. I'll still need a ride to the doctor. Sorry. I'll try to schedule the appointment so it's not such an inconvenience to you."

No matter how many times I'd seen it, the raw anger of my father being challenged made me shrink back. Before he could say anything else I apologized again and ran to my room. It was several awkward hours before he started acting like himself again; pretending we were friends while openly antagonizing and insulting me. Calling him on it was pointless and I didn't want him to take away my weekend plans. I could endure anything to get answers to my gnawing questions.

Come Saturday morning, Dad was the first one up like usual. Commitment was a core value he'd instilled in me. Even weekend plans to hangout with my friends couldn't be canceled without a good reason. Maybe he thought I'd avoid going if he didn't see me out the door. Their place was about a mile out on the opposite side of the school, but I opted to walk there myself. It might have been easier to get a ride, but suffocating in the car wouldn't do anything to ease my nerves. I needed to be calm when questioning my friends. This wouldn't be an argument like with Dad.

I felt a little lighter once I saw the familiar two-story home and Sarah sitting on the steps outside. Her arms had a few scattered bandages, but most of the cuts had healed.

Sarah nodded at my arms. "Your sleeves aren't rolled up."

I chuckled to myself that even my parents hadn't noticed the change. "Don't want my parents seeing the cuts."

"Right." A flash of sadness crossed her face, but it was gone when she stood up. "Let's get some answers, yeah?"

"Yeah."

I rang the doorbell and heard a familiar tune throughout the house. A tall woman with caramel skin and curly brown hair opened the door with a wide smile she'd passed down to her son. Veronica's muscular tattooed arms scooped me into a hug followed by Sarah.

"Come on in, kids! I guess I won't be able to call you that soon. Mmm, no I'll call you that forever." She spoke rapidly and with an intensity Ray could only wish for. It used to scare me, but now I found it comforting. "I'm sorry you all got caught up in that rift ruckus, but that's a risk warriors have to face. Luckily the suit functioned properly, even for a prototype. Though, I'm sure Eve will want to make it safer before something like that happens again."

"Wait, you know what *really* happened?" I asked.

Veronica smiled at us before opening the door to the basement. "I hoped it would happen sooner, but you know how cautious Eve is. Don't resent them for it. And make sure Ray explains everything clearly. I'll get you kids some snacks."

Ray's basement had been off limits since his father, Ori, passed away. To have his mom open the path for us felt incredibly important. I took the lead down the stairs with Sarah following a few steps behind before shutting the door. A rubbery scent assaulted my senses as I stepped into a small gym. Large pieces of equipment sat around the room with a rack of weights at one corner. The small alcove we used to play in had been converted into an arena with a padded floor and walls. A door on one side of the gym led to a small laundry room that betrayed how domestic the rest of the area used to be. Beneath the staircase was another entrance hidden from sight by wooden planks that matched the building's foundation. Ray didn't notice us approaching since he was messing with the empty right sleeve of his shirt. Meanwhile, Eve waved as if this was a normal hangout.

"Are you guys ready to explain what the hell happened on Wednesday?" I asked. "Even the GPA looked stunned by whatever that suit was."

Eve nodded. "We gave Sarah a brief rundown when we were escaping since it's about time we bring you both into this."

"I wanted to let you in on this before, but Mom convinced me I should wait til I was absolutely sure. I couldn't avoid telling Eve when she moved in," Ray explained. "You're gonna have questions, but let us just talk for a bit, alright?"

Sarah thought about it then nodded. "Yeah, deal."

All eyes fell on me, but I kept focused on Ray. We'd been friends as long as I could remember. The only other people who ever kept things from me were my parents. They would always justify it with all the awful things they imagined I'd do if I knew their secrets.

"You didn't keep it from me cuz of me, right?" I asked.

"What?" Ray was incredulous. "Dude, no. Just follow me and you'll understand."

Before I could ask anything else he opened the door and waved us inside. Credit where it was due, he was right that I understood why he might have hid it. Seeing a couple powerful computers wasn't surprising. The massive alien machine that resembled a 3D printer, on the other hand, left me gobsmacked. Sleek metal panels connected to intricate wires and cables that bound both computers to a wall of seven monitors. A long curved screen sat in the middle with two smaller ones on top and four beneath it.

"As you both know, my dad was my hero." Ray's eyes filled with pride. "He spent his free time traveling around collecting debris from rift events. This fabricator is made out of alien tech he found. He used it to make tools to help humans against the Riftwalkers. I hung out down here and pestered him to take me on one of his trips. Some of it's hazy, but I do know a Riftwalker killed him and took my arm. I couldn't come down here for almost a year after that. He died protecting me and now he can't help anyone ever again."

There was a long pause and I patted Ray's back to comfort him.

"Thanks, I'm okay," he said. "When I finally came back here, I was able to immediately understand how to operate all of it. I don't mean I can read it outright, but I use it with vibes alone. I think it has to do with the alien blood that got in my wound that day."

"Excuse me?" Sarah interjected.

"Don't worry, we'll get there." Ray approached the computer and tapped one of the three keyboards to bring the curved monitor to life. "Dad had set up some weird 3D modeling software. It took a while to get a handle on it using his old models. I wasn't comfortable making whatever I wanted until Mom gave me her blessing. As long as it would help the world at large." He turned to me. "Anand, what's the thing I won't shut up about?"

Pulling my attention from the machine was difficult. I couldn't figure out how it didn't overheat without an abundance of coolant in the room. There wasn't even a soft hum coming from the massive device. The fact that apparently Ray was using it without actually understanding it was ridiculous. None of it should function logically. It was as if our reality, as skewed as it was, had been forced into the illogic of a comic book.

I scoffed softly. "The world could use superheroes."

The lower four monitors came on, each with a turnaround of a piece of armor; a helmet, chestpiece, bracers, and boots.

"It was all theory until my parents passed away and I moved in three years ago," Eve explained. "Ray had the models, but couldn't actually get them working with the fabricator. My first encounter with Riftwalkers was... unpleasant, obviously." Eve ran a thumb along the side of her choker that hid a scar along her neck. "I got sharper afterwards. Similarly to Ray, I could understand this tech. I got the fabricator to actually work so we could test our ideas."

Eve opened the door of the fabricator to reveal a pedestal in the center holding a bionic arm. She brought it to Ray and helped him slot it onto the socket where his shoulder should be. It dawned on me that there was never any settlement. No wonder Ray never gave any details about it.

"Once we got his arm working, we realized it was possible to push forward with the Glaives. That's what we actually call the suit you wore. Gale is just the codename for yours. At first we were going to fabricate them outright, but then learned about the Riftwalkers' capacity for transformation." The display changed to monstrous diagrams, each marked by a glowing circle. "They all have this *core*. I don't know if they're born with it or if it's grafted into them, but we were able to nab some for the suits."

"Fabricator must be linked to some sort of storehouse," Sarah said.

Eve nodded. "That was our assumption, too."

"Since you guys seem to understand what's on screen, I'm assuming you might have mutated this week," Ray explained.

"Yeah, both had wounds that mixed with Riftwalker blood." Eve clarified. "Probably more than we noticed with all the running for our lives and shit."

A simple glance at the screen allowed me to understand a little bit of what the Glaive parts could do. I wasn't even reading the foreign text on the diagrams. There was just an innate understanding of what they meant. Concerns must have been racking Sarah's mind as well, but she looked as calm as ever. I wasn't freaking out, per se, but not all my questions had been answered.

"Why explain all this now?" I asked.

"It was always the plan once prototypes were tested," Ray answered. "I made suits for all of us, but was hoping not to need yours or Sarah's. Thankfully, Gale came in clutch during the anomaly."

Eve let out a dejected sigh. "I dropped the ball when it mattered."

"Don't worry about it," Ray insisted, then turned to me. "Look, I wanted to be the first to test one before giving you your prototypes. When the original plan fell through I saw no way out without putting you in danger."

"Why not take this to the GPA? They have testing facilities and probably more means to replicate it." I wanted to use the word *improve*, but Ray already looked slightly upset by the question.

"Anand, don't be stupid," Sarah said sharply. "It's not just Ray and Eve's project, but also his dad's. Course Ray wanted to be the one to test it."

"Shit, sorry. I hadn't considered that."

"It's..." Ray took a deep breath and said, "Whatever problems you have with Arjun, you'd do what was needed to keep him safe, right? If not for you, then for Priti. Kinda like that, I want to be the one to keep Dad's legacy alive. I'm not against taking it to the GPA once I'm satisfied with it. But until I am, it needs to stay between us."

I nodded slowly. I'd never really thought about it, but Ray was right, I'd do anything to keep my parents safe. Not doing so would make me a failure in my own eyes.

"How do we get to other places when rifts appear? You can't expect them to always happen nearby," I said.

"So, you're in?" Eve asked.

"No, yeah." Sarah answered immediately. "Anything for the people."

I grunted in agreement. "Not to mention, it'd be a waste to let those suits you made go to someone else."

Sarah approached the terminal and watched closely as Eve began walking through certain features. My focus remained on the Glaive diagrams. So much information was packed into the screens that I couldn't process. But the feeling of wearing one remained in my mind. The idea that I'd get to do so again both excited and terrified me. Not the fact that I'd be in danger, but that my parents might catch on. Though, in the long run, I'd be doing a service to humanity.

Ray sidled up to me and patted my shoulder. "Asking was just a formality. There was no chance you'd give up the chance to be a superhero."

"We're too old to play make-believe," I replied.

"First of all, no we're not. Secondly, that's not what I'm talking about. Your Dad's been on your case about being a doctor forever. You never complained about it until the prospect of being a GPA agent came to mind. You said something like, 'It doesn't matter what I need to do to get there, I want to help people.'"

I raised an eyebrow. "Do you memorize everything we all say?"

"When it's important." Ray shrugged. "Anyway, I knew you'd be part of the team the day I started working on the Glaives. Speaking of which."

Ray walked to the desk and pressed his metal hand into the side. Something clicked, opening a cabinet underneath. From inside he retrieved a silver bracelet and a pair of blue thick rimmed glasses.

"I call them Scabbards, they hold the Glaives. I hope the glasses are to your liking, Anand. Figured aviators everyday might be a bit much. And Sarah, you've always got some bracelets on so this one should fit right in."

There wasn't an ounce of hesitation in Sarah when she grabbed the jewelry and slipped it on. "Eve's Scabbard is the choker since she wears one everyday. What's yours?"

Ray flexed his mechanical bicep. "It's far from ordinary, but no one will bat an eye at it."

"Now you just need to unsheathe before a monster rips your arm off," Eve said.

Every one of us was well versed in curbing Ray's idiotic habits. Ambition was well and good, but without someone to reign the passionate guy in, things could get problematic. In fact, their plan for the prototype failing was surprising. Unexpected fear wasn't something either would consider. I wanted to ask Eve about it, but now wasn't the time to do so. And based on her reaction during the crisis, Ray's plan didn't involve trying to transform in the middle of an attack. It was surprising Veronica hadn't warned Eve about something like that. Maybe she thought I'd handle it moving forward.

"Any chance we can try them out?" Sarah asked.

"No..." Ray sighed.

"What do you mean?"

"We can't unsheathe outside of rift anomalies. We've tried everything and I'm guessing the Scabbards need to detect an Oghrodi to activate."

I was incredulous. "You're telling me you weren't sure I could transform yesterday?"

Ray replied sheepishly, "I was 99% sure you could."

"I was *100%* sure," Eve interjected. "Otherwise I would've argued more against it."

If Eve was sure yet still fearful, there had to be something more going on. They definitely needed more help. I finally grabbed the glasses out of Ray's waiting hand. The lenses were relatively thin compared to what I was used to yet my vison was clearer than ever. It must have had something to do with the Riftwalker core they were made from.

"Who all knows about the Glaives? Just us and Veronica?" I asked.

"Veronica just keeps it a secret. While she has contacts at the GPA, she doesn't let that interfere with us," Eve said. "She can get us in contact with them, but won't do so unless absolutely necessary. Otherwise she's just our mom."

"She wants to watch over us, got it. Different question then; what's the plan for the strip mall cameras? They had to have seen the Riftwalker and us. Even if the GPA deletes the records, they'll have seen me transform. I don't think it'd take long to figure out where to go from there."

Before either of them answered me, Eve slapped Ray's shoulder. "I told you he'd think of it!"

"I agreed with you! Someone just had to be on the other side of the bet!" Ray complained.

He turned towards the monitors and powered on the last two atop the terminal. One displayed our familiar Discord chat. The other was the Rift Report site with an extra tab open. My eyes went wide when I saw the email from Mizzek, the site's main reporter. I'd messaged them directly on their site for years and had never heard back, yet Ray and Eve managed to actually get in touch with them. Obviously, it had to do with the Glaives, the email said as much, but I couldn't deny my jealousy. Within the message was an embedded video that wouldn't play. Apparently, it only worked once, but Ray confirmed my suspicion that it was footage from the Willy Street Co-op when I transformed. The message ended with the request for a meeting in a couple weeks at the local Prairie Cafe.

"That can't be a coincidence," Sarah said. "That's your favorite brunch place."

That didn't sit right with me. I might have been the one who transformed, but the recording would at least show that the equipment was borrowed. Nonetheless, dwelling on it wouldn't help. I took the lead on replying to the email with a simple message: We'd be there.

Mysterious Informant

The daily routine I'd grown accustomed to changed to accommodate our new project. Glaives only enhanced properties that were already there. Facing a Riftwalker head on had made it clear that biweekly PE wasn't enough exercise. While Ray and Eve had used some of the equipment in their basement, we all needed a lot more practice. Thus, we committed the two hours we spent together after school to training at their house. Any time we weren't training was spent coming up with plans in case of another encounter, but I was bothered by the feeling that it may never happen again.

Rift anomalies rarely occurred consecutively in the same location. Exactly 86 rifts had ripped through the skies over the past 23 years and only seven places experienced repeats. Even then, I couldn't find a pattern for the frequency. If the GPA knew *why* the repeat anomalies happened, they hadn't shared it with the public. There was the chance that Mizzek knew something, but I wasn't even sure why they wanted to meet. I held on to my questions, but figured we should approach this like Ray and Eve's explanation of the Glaives; let Mizzek speak until they're done then press forward if we trust them.

Part of me already didn't know what to think when they invited us to a restaurant that closed long before school was out. Mizzek also somehow knew about our typical meeting window. I hoped they didn't know why. The idea that a stranger might know about my relationship with my parents was humiliating. Not to mention how disappointed they'd be in me if it reached them. That compounded with everything else on my mind until I was basically a zombie at home. But staying silent and obedient was all my parents wanted so it worked out perfectly.

When the day of the meeting arrived, I could barely focus on classes. I scoured the Rift Report forums for any information about Mizzek full well knowing they'd never let anything slip. Even the newest posts about the anomaly in Wisconsin didn't mention the Glaive. Clearly Mizzek saw some use for us or they wouldn't be keeping our secret. The GPA likely had a similar reason for never reporting on Gale. We'd searched every resource we could think of and nothing came up related to the suit. I hoped it meant Mizzek wasn't planning to blackmail us and our meeting would result in a new ally.

Prairie Cafe was normally closed after school, but when we arrived one of the employees was waiting near the door. She asked who we were and upon introducing ourselves, welcomed us in. The counter, normally lined with baked goods, was empty and no one occupied the kitchen. Everything at the

self-serve station was neatly organized for the next day's cus-
tomers. Chairs were flipped onto tables while the leathery seats
at booths were still slick from being cleaned. A carpeted section
that normally had grouped tables was rearranged into a single
long one. Four meals sat in front of empty seats. An unknown
person sat at the head of the table with their own half eaten
meal.

Their unkempt white hair parted in the middle to reveal a
long tan face with sharp features. Golden eyes shone under the
light as they intently studied us. It was difficult to read the emotion on Mizzek's placid face. Their gaze lingered. While I'd seen
many people wave someone over in my lifetime, the way Mizzek
did it was so smooth that it looked uncanny. Ray patted my back
when he noticed I hadn't moved while the others took their
seats. It wasn't hard figuring out where to sit since each setting
was someone's favorite meal from the cafe. Somehow Mizzek
knew each modification we all liked, but I worried questioning
it would put them off from sharing anything else. I just opted
to sip the coffee I brought myself.

"You may go," Mizzek said to the employee with a familiar
stoicism that put me on edge. "Introductions are in order. My
name is Mizzek. You are Anand, Sarah, Evelyn, and Raimundo."

"Just Ray is fine," the large boy replied. "And Eve too for that
matter."

Only family ever referred to Eve by her full name and no one
called Ray anything else.

Mizzek nodded, then continued. "There is no audio recording in this building so we may speak freely. As you are aware, I maintain the Rift Report website and thus have a vested interest in the effect these anomalies have on Earth. Informing the masses has been useful, but that suit you utilized is the first piece of true inspiration that has come from it. You have the capacity to train and equip yourselves, but that is where your skills end."

There was silence, but no one responded. A surprisingly soft smile appeared on Mizzek's face before they spoke again.

"I would be doing a disservice to the whole of humanity if I did not offer my assistance to those trying to save it. Aside from my capacity to bypass security systems, I have information that the Global Protection Agency would prefer stayed hidden. Making posts regarding my findings is unwise, but I can share it in person and private communication channels. That is why I called you here today." They looked around the table and chuckled once again. "I have done extensive research into each of you. Once I found the records of your visits to this establishment, I took note of your most common orders. Whether you partake or not is of no matter to me."

Something felt off about the suggestion when they hadn't eaten any more since we'd arrived. I couldn't put my finger on it and it felt silly to hesitate when Eve took a careful bite. Once she confirmed it tasted fine, the others followed suit. Still, I didn't let my eyes waver from Mizzek. From a leather satchel sitting on the floor at his side he retrieved four portfolios and passed them to each of us. Inside were detailed records about the seven locations where rift anomalies occurred in succession. A knowing look passed from Mizzek to me that made it clear they'd seen me scouring the site recently.

"You are on the right track, Anand. It is the very reason I reached out to your team. Your suits would do no good if you couldn't reach a rift anomaly. However, I can say without a doubt that the next will occur here. You see, in the past, these attacks happened when humanity revealed a new tool against the Riftwalkers. They do not know where the tools originate from and their second attack involves searching for any clues. If you look at the aftermath records, something is often stolen during these raids."

I reviewed the files carefully. A Runner from the original batch was taken and caused a change in evacuation patterns. Stolen stitchers demanded a modification in how the weapon operated. Even something as innocuous as the armor worn by GPA agents was taken. Lives were always in danger, but there was a noticeable increase during repeated anomalies. I was both impressed by the defense GPA agents put up and horrified by the amount of them that died before taking down a Riftwalker.

"The GPA gets targeted during repeat anomalies," Eve said while rifling through the papers. "Advancements that can hinder Riftwalkers typically come from them."

"Precisely. That is where my prediction stems from," Mizzek replied. "I would go so far as to say the principal rift will appear near the local GPA base when the next anomaly occurs. Given that Anand successfully defeated a Riftwalker."

I shook my head. "I wouldn't call it defeating as much as pushing it out of bounds. But I get your meaning."

"I do not think you do. Never before has humanity been able to shatter parts of a Riftwalker like you did. Not without a concentrated effort. You did so with a single strike. Those monsters will see that as a weakness to bolster. The Riftwalkers present during the raid will likely be stronger than the one you already faced."

"We haven't even gotten to practice in the Glaives yet..." Ray grumbled. "They can't activate outside of a rift anomaly."

"I could take a look at your systems if you would like."

"No." It looked like Ray surprised himself with the answer.

Eve explained for him. "We appreciate everything you've told us. We could even continue to work together against the Riftwalkers. But the Glaives are ours to maintain."

There was a brief silence as she and Ray looked at Sarah and I. Neither of us disagreed with Eve's claim, not that we could anyway. It was their project to start with and I'd always defer to them regarding who should be involved. While Mizzek didn't raise any concerns, they took a moment to process the response. I didn't think much of it since they'd been doing it this entire time. Though the longer they took, the more my mind began to wander.

Glancing out the window I could see a street that had been recently repaired after massive stones had rained down on it. The number of brand new cars parked in the lot was immediately noticeable. Many had been destroyed in the chaos. Whatever issues humans had with one another, they came together when facing the rifts. The average person had some sort of plan of action during an anomaly. Those who went above and beyond typically worked with the GPA. That was what each of my friends and I were planning; it might still be my path. But an enticing alternate option was at our fingertips.

"Ray created the Glaives as a way to carry on his dad's legacy," I said, drawing everyone's attention. "Eve is fighting back to stop anyone from losing family like she did. Sarah wants to protect people and not feel so powerless. If anything I have the weakest reason to fight in that I'm supporting their goals." I faced Mizzek and asked, "Why are you helping us and not working directly with the GPA?"

Instead of taking time to process, Mizzek let out a soft chuckle. "This is an expected inquiry. The GPA may protect citizenry, but it is secondary to their research of the rifts. You all, on the other hand, want to support the weakest of humanity for the whole to prosper. My family was lost during an anomaly and I could do nothing to protect them. They became numbers on a list of rift casualties. With each loss I have seen the light fade from humanity. Fear hangs over them like the anomalies themselves." Mizzek met my gaze then moved to everyone else before landing on Ray. "I think your belief is what aligns me most to you. The world needs superheroes. They bring a kind of hope that the GPA has never been capable of. If I could do even a small part in bringing the light back to humanity, I will have led a good life."

While I wanted to remain objective about the situation, I couldn't. There was such sincerity in Mizzek's words that my doubts fell silent. Behind the stoic face I saw the tired eyes of a person trying their hardest to push forward. For some reason I had forgotten how much I relied on them for most of my life. I basically grew up reading the Rift Report; to the point it became a core part of my identity. Joining the GPA would have never even come to my mind if not for the time I'd spent learning about anomalies from Mizzek.

Ray was the first to rise from his seat and walk towards the informant. The winning smile I'd grown accustomed to finally appeared. He stuck a hand out towards Mizzek. They reciprocated the gesture and were welcomed to our team. After shaking hands, both sat back down and Mizzek let out a long sigh. Finally, they took a bite of their goopy pancakes.

"I was so nervous I could not bring myself to eat lest I vomit."

Seeing everyone partake of the meal broke down my last concern and I took a bite out of the cold eggs benedict on my plate. It was the worst meal I'd ever had during one of the best moments of my life.

Crucial Modifications

The threat of a looming rift anomaly weighed heavily on everyone's minds. Training became more than physical. Everyone's free periods became a time to discuss privately with Mizzek. I wasn't sure what the others did, but I spent my time with the Rift Reporter getting years of questions answered. They provided every bit of information gathered about Rift-walkers that couldn't be posted online. While it was sparse, there was enough to gain a basic understanding of things they all had in common. The monsters were often over seven feet tall and had the ability to transform to some degree. Most of them summoned bestial appendages or sprouted armor. Some even went as far as mimicking humans, but, like Wendigo, they were never perfect.

The only thing keeping me grounded as the days passed was constant conversations with my friends. If they weren't nearby, they were chatting online. We put as much security in place as we could, but accepted it wasn't perfect. While we made a point of being vague about the Glaives online, we didn't avoid the topic outright.

As Ray put it, "This'll all go to the GPA eventually. Once everything is perfect."

It became a mantra of sorts. I wasn't entirely sure what "perfection" entailed, but I'd push myself to reach it. Though we couldn't advance as forcefully as we wanted. Life had to come first or none of this was worth anything. Overworking made me feel like I was becoming my father and I wanted nothing more than to avoid that. Not to mention, our general health was crucial if we wanted to actually be effective during rift anomalies.

Several days after that first meeting with Mizzek I ended up walking to Ray and Eve's alone. Ray had a doctor's appointment and Sarah had an important dinner with her dads. Eve's schedule had her home hours before me. The last remnants of snow had finally melted away and a familiar heat hung in the air. Running to my destination was a good warmup to the day's training. I didn't bother knocking on the house door, knowing it'd be unlocked since Eve was already there.

Normally she'd greet me from the basement, but it was silent when I arrived. Eve was hunched over the fabricator muttering to herself. Bloodshot eyes stared closely at the screens as she typed in illegible code. It hadn't taken long to realize that Eve had a better understanding of the Riftwalker language than any of us. That's why she handled implementing features into the Glaives. Though I worried about how much time she spent pouring over the code and adding slight modifications. At some point there would be diminishing returns; she'd just be wasting energy.

"Hey Eve, how's it going?" I asked.

Confusion was obvious on her face until she checked her phone. "Oh, I didn't realize what time it was. It's good. I'm good. Actually, it's great you're here." With each word Eve started talking faster, but it wasn't like the excitement Ray normally exuded. "This was only theoretical before, but I was able to implement it. I'm sure it'll feel uncomfortable until you get used to it. Pushing past human limits is the point of the Glaives though so not doing it would be a disservice to Ori."

"Eve, what are you talking about?"

"The instinct thing!" She paused to let her thoughts catch up.

I'd never seen her like this. Ever since the encounter with Wendigo she'd been acting off. At first I thought it was sadness at the memory of her parents, but now I could sense a palpable layer of fear beneath every word and action. I grabbed a chair from the corner, unfolded it and sat next to her. Even at her most competitive, Eve was never this nervous. In all our years of gaming together she took the role of a master tactician, reading our opponents moves and countering with ease. For her to be so distracted was off-putting.

"You mentioned your body moving faster than you could think during the Riftwalker encounter," she explained. "It looks like the Glaives can amplify mental abilities as well as physical. The new programming will let you go just that much faster and be a little bit stronger when the need arises."

"Don't you mean 'us'?" I asked. "Anytime you've brought up the Glaives recently it's with a distance. As if you aren't going to be there. But you're not the type to flake on us *or* a project you're part of."

Eve finally looked away from the computer, meeting my gaze with pain in her eyes. "I abandoned you all last time. I failed to test the prototype and you had to get in harm's way."

"I made that choice myself."

"That was too risky! It should have been me, but I just couldn't move!"

I shrugged. "Honestly, I would've probably pushed to back you up anyway."

"I didn't even think to do that!" It jarred me to hear Eve yell. "I was a coward! I'm still that kid who hid while her parents died fighting! My brain froze when I felt that rift a couple weeks ago. All the therapy and preparation went out the window. I've spent the last three years focusing on Riftwalker research and it was for nothing!" Tears flowed down Eve's face. "If you hadn't ran out of the bunker, we'd probably be mourning Sarah. And if you hadn't covered for us we might all be dead. I knew something might go wrong. I was the backup plan and I got too scared to act. I keep strengthening the suits hoping I'll feel ready, but it still hasn't happened! I don't want you guys going into this without me. But no matter how much I train or program, I'm still scared."

"We all are," I interjected.

The words seemed to knock Eve's train of thought off track. I studied her eyes and noticed a familiar twinkle. It was rare that she actually asked for help. When she did, it was always in silence. The last time was after her parents' passing and Ray took the lead then. The idea I could do this alone was laughable. But this burden had been weighing on Eve for weeks. Waiting for the whole group to plan and intervene was selfish. It was uncaring and I couldn't stand the idea of abandoning her because I was too awkward.

"It makes sense to be scared of Riftwalkers regardless of how many times you've encountered one. Fighting one might dampen the feeling, but I don't think it'll ever totally go away. I mean, it's literally a—" I threw up my hands dramatically to sell the point. "*Monster*. A monster, Eve. All we can do is train and steel ourselves. It makes sense you'd be frustrated since you normally plan for everything and come out on top."

"I *planned* for how I'd feel. I knew I'd be scared," Eve said defensively.

"Did you know *how* scared you'd be? I don't think anyone can plan for that. Tell me honestly, do you think you'll be as scared next time as you were last time?"

"No—"

The word had barely left her lips before I replied, "Wrong. You don't know. No one does. We can't know how we'll feel about something until we face it. What I *do* know is that you can still make a plan even if you're scared. None of us knew what to do with Wendigo except you. I doubt it'll be the last time we rely on your wits. I mean, that's what happened last time, right?"

Ray and Sarah had gushed about how Eve found a route out of Willy Street Co-op and kept all of them hidden during the fight. It would have been impossible to rendezvous afterwards if not for her ability to keep track of everything happening. Ray might have invented the Glaives, but Eve's ingenuity made them functional. I told her as much.

"You think too highly of me," Eve said.

I shrugged. "It's not just my opinion. It's what I've seen. You might think it's nothing, but I can't do any of that. Neither can Sarah. Ray's the closest to you in terms of using the fabricator and he mainly handles the physical designs. We're all just following your lead."

She chuckled. "Ray would hate hearing that."

"Dang, you're right. Um, Ray leads us to the fights and you lead us in them."

"That's not... Nevermind. Yeah, that'll help me stay calm," Eve said with a smile. "I'm not alone."

"You never were," I replied with my best impression of Ray's wide grin.

"Right." Eve turned back to the monitors with newfound vigor. "Alright! I think the Glaives' new baseline improvements will make us superhuman."

"Super-*heroes*. Can't let Ray catch you slipping up like that or he'll throw a tantrum."

"You really think we can be?"

We had to be. If everything Mizzek said was true, we invited danger to our home. It was the Glaives' duty to protect as many people as possible during the upcoming anomaly.

"We *will* be," I answered. "Ray once said superheroes were a symbol of hope. Their very existence lets people know everything will be okay. The GPA does good work against rifts, but a militia like that does little to put peoples' minds at ease."

Eve parroted one of Ray's favorite lines. "The Glaives, as in us, will be a lot more personable than GPA agents."

"I agree insofar as Ray oozes charisma. If anyone can be a superhero, it's that guy," I said.

Eve's usual glow had returned to her eyes. "You've got a lot of faith."

The next words out of my mouth surprised me, like years of inhibition briefly vanished. "Mom wanted me to have faith in her teachings, but they seemed like justifications for my failings. So instead I put my faith towards you, Sarah, and Ray. There's tangible evidence of the good you do."

While Eve took the information with a smile, I felt a pit in my stomach. I'd never verbally denounced either of my parents. My friends may have caught on to my issues, but that was from what they saw, never anything I said out loud. Eve must have noticed the dower look on my face because she reached over and patted my shoulder.

"Don't worry. I won't mention it," she reassured.

While I appreciated the confirmation, it didn't ease my concerns. I left my glasses with Eve and focused on exercising through the stress. Eve greeted Ray when he arrived, but I continued training in silence. He could tell something was wrong with me now, but didn't mention it. Any time the thoughts became overwhelming I just pushed myself harder. Distractions vanished in the presence of pain. My arms and legs were killing me, but I preferred that to my anxiety. Hours passed without my notice. Normally I would have stopped to collect my things and head out. What brought me out of the intense tunnel vision was the familiar ringtone I'd mapped to my parents.

I quickly collected my things and began running up the stairs as I answered. My parents had expected me home ten minutes ago. They never got a message from me about needing extra time. Mom might have been the one talking, but I could feel Dad's anger through her. I braced myself for what he would say when I got home. Maybe I could pause and think once I got to the door. That felt like a great plan until I actually arrived. They must have seen me coming up the block because my mother was waiting at the open door. She remained silent as she let me in, but I felt the incoming argument in my bones.

The door had barely shut before she cried, "Where were you? Why didn't you call?"

"I got distracted working on the project. Sorry." I hurriedly walked to the dining room where my father awaited.

"You think just because you bought a pair of glasses you're an adult? That you don't need to tell us where you are?" he asked angrily.

I had lied and told my parents I used my saved up allowance to get a pair of glasses from our local optometrist. They were too busy to confirm the truth.

"No? I just lost track of time." I answered.

"Doing what? You're covered in sweat and have nothing to show for this project you won't tell us about."

"I'm sweating because I ran home," I said weakly. "And it's not important."

"If it's not important then why are you wasting time with it when you could be doing something productive?" Dad's voice was growing louder already.

"I'm done with my homework."

"Ask for extra credit."

I couldn't stop the incredulous look on my face. "I can't? That's not how it works." Slowly, my face returned to normal and I tried reasoning with my father. "I have some extra time now and want to spend it working with my friends."

"You say 'working', but really you're just goofing off."

"Is that so bad?" I asked rather than defending myself.

"If you waste your time with your friends and don't study, you'll never be successful. Forget being a doctor, you won't be able to do anything."

"There's plenty of stuff I could do."

"No, you can't!" Dad yelled. "You don't have skills of any sort! I'm trying to help you do something worthwhile and all you do is make excuses. No more going off to your friends' after school. I want you home and studying."

"No!" I yelled back without thinking. "I'll be home on time, but I want to spend time with them. It's... all I've got."

Dad almost said something else, but Mom was first to respond. "Come home on time or call when you're running late. We were worried sick. Now, have dinner."

It felt disingenuous to hear about their worries when all Dad ever did was antagonize me. But arguing after Mom successfully stopped it would only make everything worse. And I had stupidly spoken up without thinking. They would surely discuss what I said and complain about it later. Even so, I silently sat down and scarfed down my meal. Every passing minute made it clear that I couldn't keep deflecting my goals anymore. If Project Glaive worked how we intended, I'd have a clear shot towards the GPA. My parents would be disappointed, but at this point, there was no changing that. The least I could do was follow my gut.

Hero Entrance

Making a plan to speak with my parents was a more involved task than I expected. Finding the nerves to do it was only the first hurdle and I was at a loss. Maybe that's why I felt thankful when, a few days later, my morning routine was interrupted by the horn of the GPA's rift anomaly system. The speakers erected on local street corners blared information to civilians. The cacophony reached even the most remote residential suburbs.

Mom ran down the stairs in a panic and turned to Dad for guidance. He didn't even bother looking before barking for me to join them. I was already waiting outside the front door. A rift tore apart the sky a couple blocks away, lightning crackling around it as GPA agents rushed to stitch it closed. Dad finally opened the door to find me and yelled to get moving. I stalled, but Mom wrapped a hand around my wrist and pulled.

When moving to a new neighborhood, the GPA gave people instructions of where to find a Runner during rift anomalies. Our nearest one was at the end of the street around the corner. A small crowd had already amassed as they piled into the behemoth vehicle. It took a few minutes for us to get close. While my parents focused on entering the Runner, I listened to the sounds of destruction around us. Uncomfortable static erupted a street over and a powerline crashed to the ground. Trees creaked as they fought to stay upright against the wild winds. The pocket hurricane attacking our neighborhood proved difficult to seal. Cries of panic echoed from all directions. The flood of bodies moved towards the Runner and finally wrapped my parents, pushing them inside. I slipped out of my mother's grasp and ducked out of the crowd. Enough people scattered around that no one found my actions suspicious.

Out of sight, I dove behind some nearby houses. A quick scan confirmed it was all clear. My body tingled with excitement even while I knew wearing the Glaive felt awkward. It was an out of body experience. But the others trusted me to help them and I wouldn't let their hard work go to waste.

"Unsheathe!"

The moment the transformation was completed, a voice spoke in the helmet. With each word, a small red light flashed in the periphery of the HUD.

"Gale, are you there, buddy?"

Ray's excitement was palpable. Using superhero codenames was a dream come true. And no one could argue with it since flaunting one's secret identities would be asking for trouble.

Gale answered, "Yeah. Where are you, Quake?"

"Volt and I just cleared folks out of the neighborhood. We're heading toward the library to look for stragglers," Quake replied. "No sign of any Riftwalkers yet."

A different voice spoke up, trigger a green light in the HUD. It was Jade.

"Just cleared the east edge of town and heading towards you," she said.

Gale considered his options, watching over the nearby crowd. Nearly everyone was inside the Runner. A group of GPA agents lined up on a crosswalk several streets away facing away from any rifts. It was odd since another group was actively stitching the nearest portal. Further inspection revealed a large mass approaching the first group. It marched through a cul-de-sac, easily toppling structures in its path.

Its head resembled a helmet with small slits running along the sides. Red dots moved rapidly within as they searched for a target. Bulky hooved legs carried a scaly and muscular body with arms to match. Each step it took cracked concrete. A long tail stretched from the back of its neck to the ground, leaving behind ooze and shards. It was clearly looking for a fight with whatever was able to scare off another Riftwalker.

Combat stances did little to hide the GPA agents' shaking bodies. Twitchy fingers hovered on drawn weapons. There was no telling how many times they might have faced such a monster. One agent fired a bullet, garnering the ire of their teammates. Clearly the order hadn't been given yet. The projectile pinged off the Riftwalker's arm. It flexed one leg and prepared to lunge.

Gale got into a running stance before he knew what was happening. Every bit of information he'd learned during training ran through his mind. Each Glaive had unique abilities and functions activated with a thought. A row of hooked wheels down the middle of Gale's soles spun rapidly. Every step propelled him faster than any human could ever move.

The Riftwalker stood a few yards away from the agents while Gale had to cover several blocks. Even so, when the monster landed and attacked it was met with a sturdy block from the cobalt Glaive. The impact of the punch traveled through Gale's arm, forcing him to slide sideways, but he felt little pain.

"Get back! I'll handle this!" he commanded.

There was no way to turn back and check if the agents listened while the monster stared down at him. It spread its jagged maw into an uncomfortable smile before swinging another fist. Gale blocked again, but an unseen impact on his legs toppled him. He quickly recovered to see the slimy tail whipping around with scales shooting as a rain of blades. Most of the GPA agents retreated, but one was stuck from a heavy scale staking her leg to the ground. Blood pooled around the metal spike. Until the agent was safe, Gale couldn't engage freely.

Mizzek spoke through the helmet in an oddly comforting, monotone voice. "Do not worry, Gale. Help is on the way."

With a steadying breath, Gale focused on blocking or redirecting each strike. Mighty fists slammed into his arms and body. No more attacks came from the tail, but it morphed. The length of it became thin while the end grew into a large spiked ball. Hanging dozens of feet in the air, it plummeted towards Gale. If he dodged, the GPA agent would be defenseless. One of the long spikes was nearly at Gale's head when his vision was blocked by a blur of red. A massive club struck the ball before slamming into the monster's chest. It staggered back as the weapon crashed to the ground.

The GPA agent gasped as the monstrous spike was broken with ease by her savior. Quake, the crimson Glaive, stood over her. A large breastplate covered his entire torso with a portion jutting out past his chin. Gauntlets and heavy boots protected his extremities with openings near joints revealing black fibrous armor underneath. His helmet had a triangular visor extending to the sides with red metal framing it. Three horns crested the top, the largest in the center creating a fiery crown.

With his usual charming personality, Quake lifted the agent to her feet. "You okay, miss?"

"I'll manage," she replied before limping away, a piece of the spike still in her leg.

Gale turned back to the Riftwalker, berating himself for getting distracted. He was lucky to not get hurt. Then he saw why the monster hadn't attacked. It was attempting to strike something buzzing around it to no avail. Flitting in the air was a Glaive colored like the sunrise. Using a modified jetpack, Volt was able to fly. Gray fibers covered most of her body, amber and bronze plating layered on top for protection. Intricate bracers and shin guards glowed with energy as she moved through the sky. Her helmet had a single spherical visor at the front framed by plating that wrapped around her head like a hood.

The Riftwalker slammed its tail into the ground then whipped it up to throw chunks of rubble at Volt. While they were much larger than the raining spikes, they did little to slow the flying Glaive. She flew past some, but didn't bother to get too far. Her bracers extended and transformed into long barrel cylinders. After a brief second, balls of electricity shot out. They easily disintegrated the chunks of concrete into a cloud of dust which the monster used as cover to leap at its target. It didn't get too far before metallic chains as thick as Gale's arm grasped the monster from behind and pulled it to the ground.

The serpentine metal extended from the arms of the emerald Glaive, Jade. Her slim gray suit was lined with shining purple that accentuated the green plating on her arms and legs. Metal on her torso was layered like scales with geometric engravings across them. Two large spherical turquoise lenses acted as her visor.

It didn't take long for the Riftwalker to buck against the chains and break free. Jade simply detached the lax links, causing them to quickly disappear. New ones appeared from under her bracers like coiled snakes waiting to lunge.

A menacing grumble emanated from the Riftwalker. It was a strange, inimitable noise, but for some reason he couldn't quite determine, Gale understood the message: "Thieves."

"Are the Glaives able to translate?" he asked the group.

"They shouldn't," Volt said shakily then took a deep breath. "I think it's our brains processing its language."

"It matters not." Mizzek pointed out. "Kill the monster and protect humanity."

Everyone hesitated momentarily. It was enough for the Rift-walker to pounce at Gale. He weaved into range and delivered a quick combo to its chest, but it did little damage. Quake ran around the side to grab his bat before slamming it into the monster's spine. The impact was stopped by the creature's slick tail. Jade threw a chain around one of its legs to pull it off kilter while Volt showered it in blasts. The beast's slimy shell reduced the strength of every impact. All the Glaives could do was protect themselves while looking for an opening.

Gale huffed. "Dammit! We can't stay on the defensive forever—"

"Exactly! Kill it." Mizzek interjected.

"No! But we can get a sample," Gale retorted.

"The tail," Volt instructed. "We should be able to rip it off. Impact resistance won't matter against tearing force."

The Riftwalker gurgled and whipped its tail at Quake. Normally he could have stopped the hit, but that would leave Gale with little space to move. Instead, the red warrior dodged to create an opening for his smaller friend to get out of the way. The momentum of the monster's movements forced Jade off her feet and on a crash course with Volt. They collided in the air and spun out of control.

"Quake, swap with me." Gale commanded.

The fiery Glaive got in close, blocking Gale from vision. When the Riftwalker tried to attack again it was stopped by a powerful grip. The opening allowed Gale to dash behind the creature. Once he was out of reach, Quake swung his bat into the monster's torso. After all the compounded damage it finally let out a grunt of pain. As planned, it turned its attention towards Quake and began pummeling the heavily armored warrior. He stood like an immovable wall, each attack being little more than an annoyance.

"Volt, can you mess up its footing?" Gale asked.

"On it," she replied.

Volt had recovered and transformed one blaster into an arm again to hold Jade in the air. They spun before releasing each other, sending the green Glaive sailing over the monster. She landed near Gale as a shower of lightning burst near the Riftwalker's legs. At first it tried to hold its ground, but its skin was ripped apart. Orange ichor burst from the cuts and forced the creature to try dodging while still attacking Quake. A bone-rattling roar erupted from its throat.

"More Riftwalkers are incoming. You must end it," Mizzek said.

"Shit. Where's the closest rift?" Gale asked.

"I... uh, above us?" Volt answered quizzically as she stared at a tear forming only a hundred feet above the battle. "Mizzek, any idea what's coming through?"

"No. But if you kill the creator, the rift should close by itself," they replied.

"I've got a better idea." Gale said. "We're on the clock now. Jade, throw a chain around the tail!"

Though it was slick with ooze, the tail couldn't slip off Jade's chain as it wrapped around. The Riftwalker remade its makeshift mace and swung it wildly between Jade and Gale. Luckily the transformation made it easier to tighten the chain. Gale grabbed the loose end, wrapped it around his hand and ran to one side with Jade dashing to the other. Volt's blasts were keeping it off balance and for good measure Quake cracked his bat against the monster's legs, forcing it to the ground.

Gale turned to see a group of GPA agents returning with tools he'd never seen before. It didn't seem like a threat to the Glaives, but the Riftwalker started bucking wildly. Keeping the chain in hand became difficult, but Gale refused to falter. The monster rose to its feet and kicked Quake. It jumped up towards Eve, carrying Gale and Jade with it. Blood dripped from the tail as the chain dug deeper still. Instead of attacking the flying Glaive, the monster used her as a platform to jump towards the rift.

"Volt! Shock the chain!" Jade yelled.

A blast of electricity hit the links and sent a shockwave through. The end of the monster's tail ripped off before plummeting to the ground, landing with a heavy crash. A surge of energy ran through Gale and Sarah, but dissipated harmlessly. With nothing holding it back, the Riftwalker sailed through the portal which closed almost instantly.

"We clear, Mizzek?" Quake asked.

"In that area, yes," they answered.

Gale was sure he heard disappointment in Mizzek's voice, but didn't get a chance to ask before the group of GPA agents stepped forward and trained their rifles on Quake. An agent removed his combat helmet to reveal a man with twisted black locs pulled into a ponytail and thick scars across his dark skin. His trimmed beard complimented an aggressive scowl.

"What. Are. You?" he asked in a gruff voice.

"We're superheroes!" Quake answered readily. The other Glaives joined him without hesitation though Gale was ready to rush at the GPA agent.

The agent growled. "What do you *superheroes* look like behind the masks?"

"Fear not, agent. We are as human as you. But our identities must remain secret for the sake of our loved ones," Quake said.

It took everything in Gale not to groan at Quake's practiced lines. Then again, the agent seemed to ease up just a little with each word.

"You're either incredibly childish or literal children," the agent replied. "But you saved my subordinate and retrieved part of a Riftwalker. So, thanks..."

"You can call me Quake." the red Glaive looked towards Gale and the others to answer.

When they didn't, the agent chuckled. "Looks like I won't be getting more info out of you. That's fine. Mind if I ask why you didn't kill that thing?"

"It's not what superheroes do," Gale answered. "Enough beating around the bush. Take the tail back to the GPA and get the info you need from it. We're wasting time talking to you when we could be helping more people."

"We'll do that," the agent said.

Gale was the first to step away, but no one lingered long. As soon as reports reached Mizzek, they updated the team. Another hour was spent saving civilians. Some were trapped near destructive rifts while others had missed the Runners. Luckily, nothing had been taken by the Riftwalkers. As more time passed Quake, Volt, and Jade were able to act like their usual selves even while dealing with the anomaly. Gale was solely focused on the mission, but he didn't mind hearing their calming voices. It kept his concerns at bay.

There'd never been such a sudden rift appearance. Nor one so quick to close. Mizzek's records didn't have anything similar to this even from other repeated anomalies. Maybe it was because this was the first time someone saw it. But that meant it was the fault of the Glaives. Yet they were what had defended an innocent person from being killed. Gale feared being the only thing standing in the way of such a thing.

Lessons from Elders

I t took about 45 minutes for the rift anomaly to close and another hour before all bunkers were emptied. The Glaives found an empty alley to doff their gear before anyone could identify the users. It made little sense for a codeword to be used for transformation when the equipment could be removed silently. Ray just gave the reason that it helped "get in the right mindset." Maybe he was referring to the out of body experience I kept having.

It nagged at me as I walked back home. There were no remnants of the excised tail from the Riftwalker that escaped. Every speck of blood had been washed away. Only the damage to buildings and structures remained. It would take at least two weeks for those to be repaired. Thankfully, my parents' home was still standing. That feeling quickly vanished as I entered.

"Anand! Where the hell were you?" Dad screamed as I stepped inside. "We looked for you the entire time we were at the bunker! We sent messages and called! Why didn't you respond?"

I looked at my phone, but there wasn't a single missed call. Only a text asking where I was came through a couple minutes ago and it was responded to. It wasn't unheard of for people from the same bunker to depart at different times.

"Well? Say something!" Dad barked.

"Connections in bunkers are weak so I didn't have anything before a few minutes ago. When we got in the crowd outside of the Runner, I got separated from Mom. And someone needed help getting into it, so I offered. When we got to the bunker I got lost, but found my friends." Lying was becoming uncomfortably easy when talking to my parents. "We were trying to find anyone who needed aid and get them to the GPA."

"We were worried sick! We've told you time and again to stay with us in an emergency." Dad threw up his hands dramatically. "Why did you have to go help anyone? The agents were there to do it."

"Some people were getting overlooked so…" I tried to answer.

"Stop talking back! You didn't even bother to look for us." Dad jabbed a finger at me. "You think you can do anything with your friends. But you admitted you got distracted and couldn't think to try and find us!"

"I knew you were safe," I argued more sternly.

"Stop! Talking! Back! I know you were just playing around, trying to see more about the disasters outside. Do you think you're capable of handling those things? You can't do anything without us!"

"I wasn't playing around."

"Anand, what were you doing?" Mom asked in a soft voice.

I meant to match her tone, but instead ended up yelling. "I was just trying to help people! You guys were safe!"

There was a stunned look on her face then she shook her head. A familiar disappointment entered her eyes before she turned to my father. It was his role to drag me down. Maybe he thought he was keeping me humble, but all I felt was a familiar lack of faith in me. In the potential he was always scolding me for not living up to.

"You are not capable of helping people! You will make a mistake!" Dad insisted.

"I'm not trying to do more than I'm able to." I argued back. "You're the one who says I should be a doctor some day. I'd have to be pretty smart to be someone whose entire purpose is to help others."

"You are incapable of helping others." Dad's voice shook my core. I wasn't sure if he was even yelling anymore or if all the oxygen had been sucked out of the room. "You have proven me wrong. You are a failure. You will amount to nothing."

The room was spinning. It didn't make sense for him to be this mad simply because I ran late. Hell, I wasn't actually late at all. They just didn't know exactly where I was during an emergency. One that had disrupted communication. It was beyond me to keep them comfortable at all times even if I weren't taking on the role of Glaive.

Regardless of how I felt about him, being called a failure by my own father hurt in a way that I didn't know was possible.

Tears rolled down my cheeks and I felt a weight in my throat. To make matters worse, Mom just looked away in shame. She didn't bother comforting me or quelling my father. And he looked so smugly satisfied to have shattered me. I wouldn't stand for it.

"You should be happy, then. I won't be a doctor. Don't expect me to humor it ever again. I'll join the GPA and help people in ways you can't even understand." There was a fire in my chest and my mouth moved faster than I could think. "I hope I die young. Then you won't be my father. And you won't have a failure like me for a son."

"Anand!" Mom screamed and broke the intense stare between my father and I. Of course she still came to his defense after how he treated me.

I clicked my tongue. "Whatever. I'm out of here."

"You'll still have to come back," Dad said sternly.

My head pounded every time he spoke. "No duh! But you're just gonna ignore this family in your office for the rest of the day. The least I can do is go somewhere to do the same!"

I slammed the door shut on my way out. It had been a long time since I cried in public about my family, but there was no way I was going to sit around the house while suffocating like this. No matter how hard I tried to stifle the tears, they just kept coming. Passers-by glanced at me as I rushed through the neighborhood. I was embarrassed, but they probably guessed I was mourning someone lost during the anomaly.

News about casualties wouldn't be broadcast for at least a few hours. Information had to be confirmed before the GPA would go public with anything. Looking for a distraction, I opened up the Rift Report on my phone. A few new articles had popped up from different users, but the one with the most active thread was about four colorful superheroes. It was written by Mizzek themself, but they'd avoided any identifying information. It came off like an excited GPA expert discussing their newest discovery. It permitted Mizzek to discuss what was necessary without revealing any secrets.

Eventually my tears dried, but I wanted to continue my research uninterrupted. I wandered to the library, found a secluded corner where I could be alone, and scoured the web. Astonishingly, local reports were pouring in about the Glaives. People were discussing being saved or protected. Some mentioned seeing something similar during the last anomaly. It felt good to see mostly positive sentiments about the group. Maybe it would inspire the GPA to engage with Ray and Eve's project sooner than later. While the agent we encountered wasn't exactly friendly, he was willing to work with us. That was a good first step.

Part of me wondered how my parents would feel about the Glaives. Then I remembered how much Dad complained back when I wanted to buy comics. There was a reason I mainly read them at the library or borrowed Ray's. To my parents, frivolously wasting time in fantasy worlds was the worst thing I could do.

By the time I felt satisfied with my wallowing, the sun had begun to set. It had been years since I spent a day alone at the library. But it was always for the same reason. How I dealt with my parents needed to change somehow and I had a hunch things would be different after the argument today. Dad made clear what he thought of me, and I'd declared my plans for the future. There was no going back from that.

I skulked back into the house, and made my way to the kitchen, avoiding eye contact with my parents. While everything had changed in my head, they were chatting like it was any other day. Mom had me set the table and Dad was back to talking about work. For some reason he thought it necessary to remind me I had school tomorrow. Then again, it's not like we talked about anything else. I replied with one word answers and that was good enough for them.

***

A couple days passed before the first broadcast about the Glaives. Dad and Mom sat on the couch watching the news while I was splayed out on a chair next to them. They took in the information with indifference and I had to fight to keep my interest in check. At first I questioned how WKOW knew the term we used for our suits until I saw a brief recording of someone talking to Quake. The voice modulator did a good job of hiding Ray's voice, but I could have identified him by his personality alone. It was clearly an interview conducted via phone camera by a local high schooler, but my friend treated it with the same energy a superhero should bring to every interaction.

"Are you guys Riftwalkers?" the interviewer asked.

"Not at all! We're Glaives, responsible for facing those monsters and keeping you safe!" Quake answered.

The video then changed to a different recording of the Glaives jumping across rooftops before clearing debris. There were clips of them helping people who missed Runners and patrolling different streets. It even showed the Glaives working alongside the GPA for a few moments. Unsurprisingly, there was no video of the Riftwalker battle. While the newscaster did discuss it, they apparently had no footage of the event.

"Do you think you can do that?" Dad asked with a smug look on his face.

With the most innocent face I could muster, I replied. "Huh?"

"Those are trained professionals with more determination than you've ever shown. Yet you think you can help people like they do. I can't believe you really think the GPA would want you."

I rose from my chair and deliberately turned to Mom. "You said you needed a couple groceries, right? And no one grabbed them on the way home?"

We all knew who was supposed to get them, but saying it directly would just lead to him throwing a tantrum.

"Yes, why?" Mom asked.

"I'll go. Homework's done and I've got nothing else to do."

"You only have a learner's permit. I'll come with you," Dad interjected.

"You've had me drive alone for less," I pointed out. "It's just a couple blocks. I'll be right back."

Before either could say anything else I grabbed a set of car keys off the hook near the garage and bolted out the door. They'd complain no matter what, but this was an errand they had me do solo plenty of times. I wasn't about to let Dad thwart my ploy to get a few minutes away from him. Navigating the local roads wasn't too hard, but I still felt awkward behind the wheel. I parked at Metro Market and breathed a sigh of relief. My nerves were tight after driving so I scrolled on my phone to unwind.

I don't know what it was that pulled my attention away, but I saw Mizzek exiting the nearby frozen yogurt shop. They walked nonchalantly to the back of the parking lot into a large gray van with no windows. No one seemed to notice the peculiar behavior, but I couldn't contain my curiosity. Within seconds I was at the vehicle, knocking lightly on the backdoor.

"Mizzek? It's Anand."

They opened the door an inch. "Inside, quickly."

Any idea of caution went out the window when I caught a glimpse of the high tech system hidden inside. Monitors lined the walls with a powerful computer mounted underneath. The chair in the center was connected to a rail system that allowed it to move easily between displays. A wireless keyboard was connected directly to one armrest with a ball mouse installed on the other. Local maps and scanners were displayed on some monitors while others had images of rift anomalies.

"Welcome to my home," Mizzek said.

"You live here?" I asked.

"Rather than live off the grid, I prefer to exist between the lines. Most everywhere has a strong network connection these days, and it is not difficult to find places that meet my biological needs. So why waste funds on a stationary home where the GPA might find me?"

"That... makes sense," I stuttered. "I guess this is how you keep track of everything going on during rift anomalies. Don't you get affected by the outages?"

"Not since Eve patched me into your fabricator. It is why I could track you all immediately last time," Mizzek answered. "I am on the same network that keeps your communications operational."

I was awestruck and simply nodded as I took everything in. While counting the monitors, I got distracted by the appearance of the Glaives across two of them. It was a turnaround of the suits. Details listed next to them seemed more in depth than Eve's. Maybe it was because her shorthand came from years of understanding the suits. But there was an intrigue in how Mizzek had defined their capabilities. Specifically, Gale's speed and Volt's flight were marked as the most substantial abilities afforded to any of the warriors.

I pointed to that portion of information. "What's up with that?"

Mizzek pondered for a moment then explained, "Of all the Glaive's abilities, only superspeed and flight classify as superpowers. Quake's strength may be more significant than the other Glaives, but it is underutilized. Not to mention, the general physical augments and tools used are less effective than you might think. In fact, Eve's addition of blasters to her suit actually diminishes the value of flight."

"That's absurd. She has a massive range and can stay out of reach," I countered.

"How does that help if a Riftwalker bears down on a civilian? Does it make sense for a superhero to be fighting from a distance in that case?"

"Eve wouldn't stay back."

"Are you sure about that, Anand?" Before I could answer, Mizzek continued. "What happens if Ray gets disarmed? If he decided to use a weapon, why not graft it onto the suit?"

"Jade has chains that are rooted in the suit," I reminded them.

"Those do not even classify as a weapon! If not for your aid, they would never have held down the beast you battled. No! The only proper tool is Gale. All its capabilities are built into the body. Tell me, why are the wheels on its boots built with hooks?"

"Stronger grip and they help me stay upright even if my balance is off."

"Exactly! You have thought of how to break past both human and earthly limitations. Now you must simply work past that mental block in regards to—"

I finished their sentence. "Killing the Riftwalkers."

Mizzek met my eyes and nodded. With a tap of their keyboard, multiple monitors changed to display grotesque carnage caused by Riftwalker attacks. Even the articles about Ori and the Stetsons' deaths were on screen. The images reminded me of what I'd seen in Room and Board. Buildings and structures weren't the only things crushed by the aliens terrorizing our planet.

"I can't just take someone's life. It doesn't matter if they're not human," I argued.

"It should," Mizzek said while studying my face. "You are holding yourself back due to others' ideals. Your parents, Ray, Eve, Sarah; None of them should define what you can do."

"It's not them. *I* don't want to do it. I'm not ready."

"What do you need to become ready? Must one of your family die for you to need revenge?!" Mizzek's voice cracked. "Ray is seemingly incapable of anger. Eve may push past fear, but the presence of it will keep her from ending these monsters. Sarah equipped herself solely for capture and protection. I have no expectations of any of them. But you, Anand, are willing to get in close and fight. Your suit is an evolution of humanity in a way the Riftwalkers could have never seen coming. The potential for you to truly overpower one is present. I believe in you."

I hated how good it felt hearing those words in this context. But Gale wasn't me. Gale was a superhero created by my best friend to protect humanity. Eve had modified it to suit what I was capable of. The superspeed only happened because Sarah mentioned the need to get in close after I used the prototype. People I cared about invented Gale, I had no right to dirty its hands to feed my ego.

But this wasn't a simple request Mizzek was making either. This was the most heated I'd ever seen them. Their ever-present monotone was drowned in a sea of rage and sorrow. Calmness had no place in the storm of emotions washing over them. Even in the silence I could see Mizzek jittering anxiously while waiting for my response.

"Who did you lose?" I asked.

"My family. Blood and bonds were nothing in the face of those things," Mizzek answsered. "I... I am sorry, Anand. I should not push like this. For years, I have wanted to do more, but I should not foist that on you children."

It felt weird getting an apology from an adult. So much so that I stood there dumbfounded as my new friend wept at the memory of those they had lost. After several seconds, I awkwardly patted their shoulder.

"Pardon me, Anand. I need some time to myself." Mizzek opened the door for me. "I will be in touch when needed."

I waved goodbye. "Yeah, talk later."

My head felt fuzzy as I walked into the store to finally complete my errand. I couldn't imagine what Mizzek had gone through. But if they had lost everyone they ever knew, it was no wonder they were so gung-ho about killing Riftwalkers. Maybe they were right that I couldn't commit to it because I hadn't lost anyone. But I was close to Ori. I'd spent many weekends at Eve's old home with the Stetsons. Their loss still hurt me yet I couldn't bring myself to justify killing. With everything we were dealing with, I felt like something must be wrong with me for feeling that way.

Voice of Reason

Everything was a mess in my head for days. The talks with my father and Mizzek had muddled into a spiral of constant doubts. Nightmares where a multiheaded Riftwalker was berating me became commonplace. It twisted their words to paint me as a failure in every endeavor I attempted. Nothing I'd ever done would amount to anything. I couldn't commit myself fully to a single thing until it was too late. The very idea that my hesitation might cost someone else their life was stomach turning.

But the idea that I could only find success against the Riftwalkers by killing them was sickening. Regardless of what I said to Dad, I wasn't sure if I had a death wish. That in itself might be a problem, but I couldn't bring myself to discuss it. The compounding exhaustion and doubts made it hard to speak with anyone. Keeping quiet at home was welcome, but now I was worried about saying something insane in public. It wasn't a worry about how other random people might react, but rather a concern of how my friends could feel. While trying to guess their emotions, I ended up avoiding them completely.

Using my locker was a stealth mission since Ray, Eve, Sarah or some combination of the three was always waiting nearby. I arrived in shared classes late and snuck out before they could catch me. Ray wasn't around to guide me through crowded halls, but I still had the option to weave. Training to do so in combat had only made it easier. There was no way the avoidance could last if we were supposed to be a functional team. But asking my friends if killing was okay wasn't something I could do. I knew none of them would be up for it. And how would I start that conversation? There wasn't even a different topic that easily transitioned to it. We barely spoke during training so bringing it up then was a no go. Not to mention I'd skipped out for several days without warning.

Since everyone knew about my usual haunts, I resorted to wasting time in an old park near my neighborhood. We hadn't been there as a group for almost a decade, but I still dropped by alone from time to time. Mainly when I needed to think without interruption. Most of the parents there didn't mind a high schooler they recognized as long as I kept to myself. Today, thankfully, no one was around so I was able to sit on the swings and focus. At least I thought so.

"This seat taken?" Sarah asked as she sat in the swing next to me.

"You're skipping training?" I replied.

"You really one to talk?"

I let out a long breath. "Guess not. What are you doing here?"

"I was babysitting my cousin yesterday. His family lives over there." She nodded to a house nearby. "Imagine my surprise when I see you sitting on the bench with the weight of the world on your shoulders. When you left yesterday, it didn't seem any lighter. Figured you'd come back here."

"I've just got a lot on my mind."

"We noticed. Doesn't explain why you're avoiding us."

"So you came to interrogate me? Alone?"

"No, I came to lend you an ear," Sarah answered softly. "If all three of us had, you would've run."

I cracked a smile. "Yeah."

"First time you've smiled since the rift. That weighing on you?"

"No. I mean, kinda." After a brief pause I explained my conversation with Mizzek. "And that came right after a fight with my Dad. According to him, I'm a failure who's not gonna amount to anything."

"He actually said that?" Sarah asked with a hint of anger.

"Yeah. Don't believe me?" I asked.

"No, it's not that. You don't normally talk about your Dad outright like that."

Normally that would have given me pause, but I found myself failing to care. Dad already thought poorly of my friends. It didn't matter if they knew what he was like.

"I guess I don't. Anyway, after he and Mizzek talked to me... I'm at a bit of a loss." I let out a heavy sigh. "I've been having a hard time sleeping. It's like..."

"Everyone sees you one way, but that's not how you see your-self."

I stared at Sarah with a dumbfounded look on my face. "Yeah, exactly."

"My dads put me in therapy during middle school. Helped a ton with the whole 'uprooting my life' thing," she explained.

"But I couldn't put that into words."

"Sure, but it's written all over your face. Whatever you're feeling is *always* on your face."

My cheeks burned and I blurted out, "That's not true."

Sarah rolled her eyes. "All I'm saying is the Anand that spends time with Ray, Eve, and me is the one that seems happiest. Doesn't matter what your Dad thinks of you. You define your-self with your actions. No one else should be deciding what you do, not even the Rift Reporter. Ray *asked* you to be a Glaive. Eve *asked* for suggestions on improvements. You act on things because it feels right."

"That's not always true."

"Has been since we met. You told me your parents were always weird about you befriending girls. Eve got a pass since the Stetsons were old buddies of your Dad's, but your only other friends were Ray and other guys. When I moved here and knew no one, you were the one who invited me to hang out with you three. Not Ray. Not Eve. You; against your parent's wishes. I know they like me now, but that only happened because you did right by me."

Honestly, it wasn't much of a memory to me. Sarah was a new kid in our elementary school and happened to be alone at the playground. We needed a fourth person for something. I couldn't even remember the game. Sarah was so cool yet spent a lot of time alone. Which had always perplexed me given how friendly she was. I wasn't surprised that her primary instinct during a rift anomaly was to save others. If people knew how beautiful the person behind Jade's mask was they'd fall for her instantly, and likely join the ever-growing Rejected-by-Sarah Club.

"I don't always act on impulse," I said.

Sarah squinted at me and slapped my arm hard. "Yeah, it's really annoying. But it's fine since it's you being you. Don't mind as long as I can read your face. If all else fails, Ray can translate everything you're thinking."

I looked back at her with what I hoped was a neutral face. "So I'm not wrong for pulling away from my parents? It doesn't make me a bad son?"

"I'll be real: you might in their books. I don't think you are. They want you to have good grades and be healthy. You're doing those things. At most you're just getting off the doctor path route Dad's been raving about. Instead, the world is getting a superhero. Huge win in my book."

"I'm not even sure if that's viable. How would I make money? Would it be possible once we start working with the GPA? What if they have demands I don't agree with?"

"Keep acting like yourself, duh. Things have a way of working out when people do that." Sarah gave me a wide smile and I felt a blush on my cheeks.

The swing started to sway as I finally moved my legs. For the first time in a while my head was empty. All I was concerned with was how nice the sky looked and how much my friends had worried about me. Some part of my brain was trying to dig into everything Sarah said, but I knew I wasn't equipped for that. Maybe I'd bring it up with Ray eventually. He'd get a kick out of it at least.

"Thanks for talking me through the funk," I said.

"No problem. Would've been easier if you hadn't avoided us for days," Sarah replied with a smarmy grin. "Remember that for me next time."

"Yeah. I'll apologize to the others when I get a chance."

Sarah's phone had begun ringing, but she waited for me to finish before answering. I noticed it was Ray and the call was quickly put on speaker. We knew something was wrong from the tone of his voice.

"You guys are still together? Good. Something's wrong. There's rifts popping up around the city." Ray's connection became fuzzy as the emergency siren rang out across the neighborhood. "Can you... hear me? Shit! Our connection should be stable."

"We hear you. What's the plan?" I asked.

"Get some privacy, unsheathe, and help anyone you can. We'll meet up when possible."

"Roger!"

Sarah hung up and dashed out of the park with me a few steps behind. We hopped the fence into her aunt's backyard and crouched near the tree. Sarah forcefully moved her hand in front of her face, the Scabbard jingling down her arm before transforming into her Glaive. It was surprising to see her pose for the transformation like Ray had suggested during training. I simply uttered the codeword and waited for the inevitable disconnect of my mind and body as Gale took charge.

The first goal was to get everyone out of the neighborhood. It was surreal to be treated like celebrities by those who had seen news about the Glaives. Excitement quickly turned to panic as it dawned on civilians why the warriors might be knocking on their doors. The anomaly siren sounded several minutes late. The GPA clearly hadn't seen this coming. The sudden disaster caused more hysteria than any Gale had seen before.

Worse yet, Mizzek was unreachable for information. Thankfully, finding people who were trapped was possible without them. Volt upgraded the detection system in the Glaives which allowed for real time mapping via vibrations. The topographical map in the HUD corner didn't track life-forms, but with the Glaives' enhanced senses it didn't have to. Even without visual confirmation it was possible to tell where people were gathered. It didn't take long to clear out the area and guide the residents to the nearest Runner.

"Hey, Glaives," a GPA agent yelled to Gale and Jade. "We've got reports about trouble at Greenway Station. Think you can head over there?"

"We're on it," Gale replied.

There was no reason to challenge it. The GPA knew their strengths and struggles. If they were having trouble, it was likely related to a Riftwalker. Helping them handle this was the perfect show of comradery and another step towards officially teaming up with the organization. With enhanced movements the Glaives could travel miles much faster than a human. The giant Runners had a lot more trouble navigating between abandoned vehicles than the armored duo. Gale and Jade quickly left the neighborhood, but couldn't ignore the issues slowing down evacuation. Agents pushed cars aside to make room, but it took several people to move one.

"Gale, you're faster than me. Head to Greenway Station. I'll help here and catch up." Jade said.

"If I'm faster, shouldn't *I* help, then catch up?" Gale challenged.

"I basically have extra hands." Half a dozen chains sprouted from Jade's forearms and latched onto nearby cars. "Gotta finesse it so they don't get too damaged."

With an effortful grunt, she shoved multiple cars aside. Nearby agents took notice and made space for Jade to work. It was important that Gale trust his ally to handle this alone. There was no telling what was going on at the station. His treads revved and he launched into a superhuman sprint. To anyone else, he must have looked like a metallic-blue blur. They couldn't make out the details like his spinning treads and specific movements that compounded into superspeed. But to Gale, the world around him looked perfectly still. Even hurried Runners were sluggish in his mind. It was as if, somehow, his brain had accelerated to keep up with his body.

With the addition of a few shortcuts, Gale covered the three mile trip in one minute. Greenway Station was an outdoor shopping area with tightly packed buildings surrounding a large parking lot. The perfect place for multiple Runners to pick up a crowd before transporting them to a bunker further out of town. Gale arrived to see a massive group of civilians cowering behind ten GPA agents holding the line against an encroaching Riftwalker.

Its body made for an odd contrast to the last one. Legs covered in matted fur were held aloft by muscular paws and jagged claws. Its stone body wielded long tentacles in place of arms. A gross amalgamation of feline eyes and ears sat above a rocky head.

"Got a Riftwalker." Gale informed the team.

"Name?" Quake asked. He made a point that it was needed for their records moving forward. The last one they fought got dubbed 'Basilisk'.

"Uh... You're normally better at this." Gale replied. "Golem? I feel like that's accurate."

"Think you can handle Golem?"

The answer came out without thought: "Yes."

Gale surged towards the monster. He leapt over the crowd and agents, landing with a thud in front of them. A blinding glare reflected off the electric blue lens of the hero's helmet. The monster groaned in annoyance and held up a tentacle to block the light. Using the distraction, Gale planted both feet in a solid fighting stance. His treads revved and he launched forward. A solid blow cracked Golem's stony body, yet there was neither flesh nor muscle beneath the damaged layer.

The Riftwalker leapt back and balanced on the thick pads of one of its tentacles. It sprung off, allowing for a powerful roundhouse to cut across the metal on Gale's arm. The ear grating scrape was like nails on a chalkboard, but he remained steady. While his suit was visibly scratched, the damage was minimal. Unfortunately, it was impossible to dodge every strike.

Golem barreled towards the agents. Gale dashed at the monster and grabbed its flailing tentacle, crushing it in his grip. Turning in the middle of the strike, he swung the beast and sent it flying towards a wide street between two stores.

Coral blood trickled off the damaged tendril, but Golem didn't seem to care. It launched off the limb again, spinning through the air. A wheel of death targeting Gale. He looked for an opening and found a lone rift hanging high above a Michaels.

The whirlwind of tentacles thankfully swiped harmlessly off Gale's helmet, but the accompanying axe kick struck true. It slammed into the Glaive's shoulder, forcing him to crouch. Claws dug into the plated armor, but stopped before cutting into the fiber below. Once Gale found his footing, he wrapped his arms around the monster's torso and pushed forward with all his strength. Golem flailed wildly, striking Gale with its tentacles, but unable to stop the advance.

There was no telling if the next part would work, but hesitation had no place on the battlefield. Gale leapt off the ground, twisting in midair so his boots connected with the outer wall of the Michaels. It was impossible to jump again, but Gale was able to angle himself to launch off the edge of the roof. Unfortunately, every direction he could reach would still miss the rift by a wide margin. At least he could get the monster away from the crowd and think of a different plan.

"Gotcha, Gale!" Jade yelled.

Chains wrapped around his torso, rattling loosely until he reached the top of the building and leapt off. After sailing several yards, the chains tightened and forced him sideways with centripetal force. Jade's steady stance made the trip towards the rift smooth. When Gale was a few yards away, he released Golem. No amount of flailing could stop its trajectory. Simultaneously, Jade pulled back her chains so Gale wasn't lost. The rift vanished as soon as Golem went through.

It was weird that no GPA members needed to assist in sealing the portal. It didn't appear suddenly like Basilisk's yet vanished just as fast. Gale was just thankful it was gone so he could focus on how to safely return to the ground. Suddenly, the white panels on the back of his shins opened to reveal glowing thrusters. Compressed air blasted out and slowed his descent before closing again. Upon landing, Jade released him from the makeshift harness.

"We just defeated a Riftwalker!" Volt's voice rang out over the comms.

"Us too!" Jade replied excitedly. "Where do we meet from here?"

Quake hummed. "I don't think we need to. Look at the sky."

Rifts across the city were closing on their own. Pocketed disasters ended abruptly, leaving the least damaged aftermath in recorded history. More agents were freed up to aid in getting civilians back to their homes. The Glaives swept over Madison and its suburbs but found no more Riftwalkers. Some civilians thanked them for their aid while others cheered at the sight of the armored superheroes. Gale was ready to call it a day, but Quake insisted they interact with their fans. Becoming a symbol of hope involved building trust and that was best done in person Thankfully, no one could see the grumpy face behind Gale's mask as he posed for pictures. Almost a whole hour passed before the team could finally retreat to their base of operations and doff their gear.

"Do you think we had something to do with how short that anomaly was?" Ray asked the group but looked at me.

"Kinda. I wouldn't say we were the sole reason," I replied. "By the way, some *things* showed up on my legs. Like thrusters."

Eve perked up. "Oh, those are all over your suit, actually. Did you just notice? There's an air collection and compression system built into Gale that empowers your physical movements. You used them around Basilisk."

I hadn't realized while weaving around the slimy Riftwalker that my air mobility was unique to the others. "What made you think of that?"

"Ray said it suited someone who was trying to fight bare handed," Eve explained.

Sarah cocked an eyebrow at the large boy. "You sell that as an original idea?"

"Nah, but Eve doesn't care about karate bugmen. Anand does," Ray replied.

My phone kept buzzing, so I simply shrugged in response to my friend before picking up.

"Anand, please come home. Something is wrong." The amount of panic in Mom's voice made it obvious this wasn't related to our usual issues. She needed me.

"I'm on my way." I was halfway out of my seat before the words came out.

I bolted up the stairs without an explanation. The others witnessed my face, but none of them had a chance to ask questions before I left Ray and Eve's house.

Training was paying off in ways I never expected. Within ten minutes I was fiddling with my keys to get inside. It didn't matter as Mom opened the door and pulled me into a tight hug, her face and voice thick with tears

"*Aa gaya, beta,*" she croaked.

"Mom, what happened?" I asked.

She was shaking feverishly and Dad was nowhere to be found. My heart pounded like crazy and it wasn't from the workout. A severe chill ran down my spine.

"Tell me, are *you* okay?" Mom asked.

"Yeah, obviously. You don't need to worry about me," I answered. "*What happened?*"

"You're right. I can't help, but worry..." She let out a heavy sigh. "I haven't heard from Dad. I couldn't reach anyone at his office either. I don't know what to do."

The pounding in my chest rose to my head. I situated Mom on the couch, then began to pace the room. For nearly a minute, the only sounds were my light footsteps.

"Okay. Okay... Mom, get some rest," I instructed. "I'm sure Dad is just busy or maybe had to deal with the GPA. If he's not here in the morning, I'll reach out to them."

"What about school?" Mom asked.

"*Ma*, figuring out what happened to Dad is more important than one day of school. Either way I'd be distracted all day. I'll worry if we can't find him."

Mom nodded and wrapped me in a hug. "Okay, make sure to get some rest tonight. I love you."

"I know," I replied softly. "Love you too."

Mom continued crying as she retreated to her room. Today had been a normal work day. Dad went to the office and likely got in a Runner. GPA agents were good at their jobs. Even if they got hurt, civilians were kept safe. I struggled to reason with myself and focus. With a deep sigh, I made my way upstairs and stumbled into bed. All the excitement from a successful mission was long gone. There was no way to know what happened to Dad, but my brain wouldn't shut up. All I could do now was wait.

Vanishing Act

There was no reason to call about my absence since school had been cancelled anyway. Aftermath reports presented in the morning were dire. What we assumed was a victory was anything but. Minutes before Golem was defeated, an entire Runner full of civilians and GPA members was taken through a portal. My father and his colleagues, along with nearly 200 other people, had vanished in an instant. Demands for solutions poured in at the GPA. Families protested outside the local base, blaming the organization for not doing enough to protect those who were taken. But I'd seen firsthand how willing agents were to lay their lives on the line for people.

still no word from Mizzek. i think he was on the taken runner -Ray

Thanks! My day was going too well and this really brought me down to Earth -Anand sorry dude. had to let u guys know -Ray

No, yeah. Sorry. It's not your fault everything sucks right now -Anand

How's Priti doing -Sarah

Watching the news again. Bouncing between anger and crying. She keeps getting upset that I want to join the GPA,
but her heart's not in it to fight right now
-Anand

That's rough -Sarah

How are Mike and Lou? And Veronica?
-Anand

Stress baking -Sarah

Probably gonna bring a care package
over later -Sarah

Veronica's doing the same. Not baking,
but prepping to come help. -Eve

I appreciate y'all. Keep us posted if anything happens with the Glaives -Anand

dont think well need to -Ray

The doorbell rang and Mom went to answer it. Moments later she returned to the kitchen, a GPA agent in tow. He wore a crisp uniform jacket emblazoned with the GPA logo, rather than the combat gear worn during anomalies. With each confident step I recognized his familiar form and felt a pit in my stomach. It was the agent who retrieved Basilisk's tail. Though his scars made him look severe, there was no scowl on his face now. Rather, the man carried himself somberly as he sat at our dinner table. Mom gestured for me to sit across from him while she gathered some snacks.

"Good afternoon. You must be Anand," he said calmly. "My name is Alec Daniels. I'm a captain with the Global Protection Agency. I've come to apologize for our failings regarding Mr. Desai's disappearance as well as to inform you of our plans moving forward."

Mom set a tray of chai between us and sat next to me. "I do not blame you for what happened to Arjun. I have seen the hard work your group does to keep us safe. This unfortunate event hasn't changed that."

It surprised me how calm she was even though she was falling apart not ten minutes ago.

"You're one of the few people affected who feel that way." Agent Daniels took a slow sip of his chai.

"I must say, you don't look much older than Anand," Mom said softly.

He chuckled. "I'm more than a decade older than him, with experience to show for it. But I'm used to many people using my age as a way to diminish my accomplishments. People have always been adept at finding a reason to not take me seriously."

"The people saying it must be older than you."

"Exactly. I can't do anything about what others say. I can only make sure I do my job properly. Regarding that, I assure you, we will get your husband, and everyone else, back safely."

"You're surprisingly calm," Mom said.

Agent Daniels shook his head and explained, "I've simply moved past the initial panic I felt after hearing the news. One should not succumb to emotions during moments of high stress. Don't you agree?"

Mom sighed heavily and nodded. I should have known she could hold back her feelings even when she wanted to drown in them. It dawned on me that she might have been doing just that during all of Dad's tirades. It didn't excuse her standing by and letting me take it, but I did understand why she did it. After all, I was no different.

The agent's demeanor softened. "Mrs. Desai, if you had the ability to change the outcome of a situation, what would you do?"

"It would depend on the situation," she answered. "And what you asked of me."

"Saving hundreds of lives." Agent Daniels turned to me. "What we are asking for is your son's aid."

I shouldn't have been surprised that the GPA knew about the Glaives' identities. It was foolish to think Mizzek was the sole reason we hadn't been discovered. The GPA was just humoring us until we were needed.

"He would still attend classes, but all his time outside school would be spent at a GPA facility until we retrieve the lost Runner and its occupants," Agent Daniels explained. "He and his friends will be housed and fed. We want you to know he would be taken care of and with people you trust."

Mom furrowed her brow. "What exactly can my little boy do for your organization?"

The agent's eyes met mine and I silently begged him not to reveal my secret.

"The project he and his friends were working on will aid in our mission. We can improve its capabilities. Their knowledge is needed to operate it," he answered.

"I don't even know what's going on with that project." Mom took a deep breath to stay calm. "Working with the GPA involves risking his life. I'm not willing to make that sacrifice and Arjun wouldn't either."

"My team and I will be there to support Anand. We will train him and his friends to protect themselves, but they will never be put near the frontlines." Agent Daniels made brief eye contact with me and I knew he was lying.

There was a long silence as Mom sipped her chai. She looked at me, then the ceiling, then a framed picture of our family on the wall. I'd never cared for it since I thought I looked like a dork in the photo, but Mom had a giant smile. Even Dad was grinning in the picture.

Finally, she spoke up. "What kind of parent would I be if I let my son do this?"

My immediate thought was that she would prove that she believed in me. But I had a hunch that speaking up now would do more harm than good.

"One who believes in her son," Agent Daniels answered. It took every bit of strength I had not to let my surprise show on my face.

Mom hummed. "Does your mother believe in you?"

"She did. My parents passed away a long time ago."

"Oh." Mom frowned. "I'm sorry."

Agent Daniels waved his hand and brushed off the response. "Don't worry about it. I'm not here to talk about myself. I'm here to ask you to let Anand help us. I need him. He—"

"Has potential?" Mom offered.

"Yes."

"We've always said that. Maybe we were wrong about where that potential would lead."

"From my understanding, he does his best to be better everyday. That kind of attitude will go far on our team." Agent Daniels put his hands on the table. "Please, Mrs. Desai."

"Even if I say no, he'll go behind my back and join you," Mom replied sadly while looking at me. I couldn't meet her gaze.

"But his heart won't be in it without your approval. He needs to know that you trust him."

The declaration hung in the air as both of them looked at me. I awkwardly stared at the table and twiddled my thumbs. Even after all the lying I'd done over the years, this felt crazy. There wasn't a doubt in my mind that the GPA needed help from the Glaives. Every part of my being wanted to do it. My reckless actions had led to a dream come true. But guilt gnawed at my gut about the circumstances. If anything went wrong, Mom's worst nightmare would come true. I dared to glance at her and couldn't hide my surprise. There was a look of pride I rarely saw. It happened once when I had straight As. And another time when I'd gotten some accolade for boxing.

"I don't know what you've done, but the world is calling for you." Her voice was choked up. "Pack well. Focus on your training. Extra hard until this job is done, okay? Tell me all about it when you can."

I tried to think of something to say, but could only muster a quiet, "Yeah."

Moving away from the table to go to my room was a blur. The suitcase I'd only used once for family vacations was shoved in the corner of my closet. It was now storage for some old outfits I never wore. I dumped everything out before tossing in all the clothes that could fit. Whatever else I needed was in my backpack. By the time I got back downstairs, Mom was waiting with a golden plate holding a lit diya and chandan. The stuff she used during major Hindu prayers. She marked my forehead with the sandalwood paste and prayed quietly before kissing my cheek.

"Be good. I love you."

"I know," I replied like usual. "Love you too."

For the first time I actually understood Mom's intentions. A feeling that I couldn't put into words.

Agent Daniels was waiting for me outside in a black sedan. After stowing my things in the trunk, I got in the backseat.

"Did she say something while I was packing?" I asked.

"She made her wishes clear," Agent Daniels answered. "Now, let's have an honest conversation."

Collaborative Effort

The GPA had kept extensive records of everything regarding the Glaives ever since the first piece was fabricated. According to them, alien technology couldn't be used anywhere on the planet without their knowledge. They would have taken the equipment and suits right then if not for the director of the GPA herself; Jillian Graves was a fierce woman who defended the Earth during the initial rift anomaly that stretched across several continents. The very idea of her felt like a myth, but there she was, at the head of a conference table occupied by my friends and I. Her uniform covered in medals, she shone like the very beacon of hope Ray aspired to be. Scars and muscle spoke to years of battle experience. Her aura was different from any of the other agents that stood around us.

"Do you prefer being addressed by your names or code-names?" Director Graves asked me.

"Um, Ray made the project. It's really up to him." I replied.

"From our records, Raimundo, Evelyn, and Sarah all defer to you for direction. Are we incorrect?"

I tried to remember times when that had happened, but was overwhelmed by all the eyes on me.

"You're not wrong, but Anand's a work in progress," Ray said nonchalantly. "Our names work. Though I prefer Ray and she prefers Eve."

"Understood, thank you," Director Graves momentarily, as if filing away the information. "Firstly, I would like to commend your creations. They function far better than we had anticipated during your initial drafting. It is in no small part due to each of your individual bravery when facing off against the Riftwalkers. Before I continue, I must ask one more time. Are you all willing to aid us with our retrieval efforts?"

"Will this lead to a future position in the GPA?" Sarah asked.

"If all goes well, yes."

All of us were surprised by the immediate confirmation. We looked between each other for any hesitation, but were on the same page.

"We're in," I answered. "I already have personal stakes in this anyway."

"And if he does, so do we." Eve added.

Director Graves nodded, then lifted a small tablet off the table. A screen behind her came to life with images mirrored from the smaller device. Crisp photographs and videos of Riftwalkers were plastered across it with an unfamiliar word at the top; *Oghrodi*.

"While I commend everything you've done, it is clear you are ill informed about your suits. Specifically, how the Scabbards function." There was a brief pause as the director remembered the word, but she hid it well. "Riftwalker is a borrowed term from the public. Through countless missions we have learned what they call themselves: Oghrodi." The videos changed to show different battles since the initial rift anomaly. Many showed GPA agents felled by the intergalactic monsters. "As you are aware, your Scabbards are made of Oghrodi cores. The organ that allows for transformation. What you lack is an understanding of *why* they allow you to transform. "

Four almost identical images of an eagle eye view of Madison, Wisconsin appeared on screen. The first looked like a detailed map from a year before the first rift anomaly. The second image was from a year after. This picture had faint, scattered white particles. Another from a few months ago had significantly more specks on it. The last picture was covered in the oddity and dated to the exact time of yesterday's rift anomaly.

"When the rifts appeared, our atmosphere permanently changed," Director Graves explained. "These spots are known as cahlium molecules. Every passing year, the air grows denser with their presence. The density spikes during rift anomalies. Our organization is still researching if they are harmful. What we are sure of is their part in empowering the Oghrodi, and in turn, the Glaives."

"I assume they have some part in how my programming translates to the Glaives abilities," Eve pondered.

"Precisely. Your programming defines the cahlium's manifestation limits. It is also why Oghrodi have limited transformations like the slick one's spiked tail and the white one's claws."

"Basilisk and Wendigo. We name them to keep track of what we've faced," Eve explained.

"Hold on." I interrupted and questioned Director Graves. "Based on everything you're saying, does that mean the Mutant Generation Theory is real?"

She seemed surprised. "Ah, yes. You obsessively read the Rift Report. For those of you unaware, there is a theory that humans born after the first rift anomaly are different from those born before. I can confirm it is because of the presence of cahlium molecules in your blood."

"By that definition..." I sighed. "We're basically Oghrodi."

The words hung in the air. I looked at each of my friends. Eve seemed to be handling it the best. Maybe she already had a hunch about it. There was some definite worry in Sarah's eyes as she looked at her hands. Weirdest of all, Ray bounced between concern and excitement, the awkward tilt of his mouth finally settling on a smile.

"The heart of a human is what makes a superhero. It doesn't matter if we're mutants." Ray said. "Most everyone we know must have these molecules. Nothing's actually changed."

The words seemed to instantly settle any nerves Eve and Sarah had. For some reason, I didn't really care either way. Being able to transform had always been a mystery and learning why it worked was nice. That's all there was to it, though. Some part of me wondered why mutations in humanity were kept secret, but knowing that wouldn't help with the mission. It was above my pay grade and that was fine.

I continued. "Okay. So we know why Eve needs to program our Glaives and why Ray has to model them. I'm guessing our ability to transform is the reason four teenagers are being called up to help the GPA. None of you are able to use the Glaives."

"An accurate deduction," Director Graves said.

"So, what's the actual plan?"

Director Graves tapped her tablet again and revealed images of an Oghrodi skeleton with a single part lit up. "This is the core that you utilize as Scabbards." With another tap she lit up a different region. "Some Oghrodi have a similar organ we have dubbed a beacon. When activated, it can open and close a rift. We are currently in the process of controlling one so we can create a large enough portal to send in a retrieval team."

"That's us," Ray said.

"No. We are currently unaware of exactly where the rifts lead except that it is the Oghrodi's domain. You four will be stationed in the backline, helping defend the beacon we use. The Glaives are strong enough to hold the line so more agents will be free to face whatever comes through the rift."

"A battle against monsters on Earth, while a separate team searches for the lost civilians," I grumbled. "It's suicide without the Glaives."

Sarah raised her hand. "Where exactly is this happening? You can't be suggesting we sacrifice a city to do it. Think of what happened... Oh. We're gonna use Nebraska, aren't we?"

During the original rift anomaly, the entire state had been eradicated. Other countries lost similarly sized chunks of land. Massive walls engraved with the names of the fallen surrounded each perimeter to keep people out. Most structures were reduced to rubble along with any occupants unlucky enough to be around. Rumors suggested there were underground GPA facilities within the walls, but the landscape itself was desolate.

"You mentioned you're still working on stabilizing a large portal. What are we going to do in the meantime?" Eve asked.

"We have reached the crux of why you were called upon so soon. Firstly, your fabricator triggers our radar so we worry it will draw Oghrodi attention. There is no pattern to their attacks and we cannot risk letting it remain off GPA grounds. We will move the device to a designated space in the Madison base with restricted access." Director Graves nodded to the other agents. "Secondly, you lack proper training. Agent Daniels has offered to help you fill in the gaps."

"On top of our usual classes," Ray grumbled.

Agent Daniels snorted. "Can't have you kids failing out while playing heroes."

"*Super*-heroes. And so far we've done everything we set out to do. Including, apparently, impressing you guys enough to come to us for help."

"I can't deny that," Agent Daniels replied. "Tell me, what's that designation got to do with training?"

"It means we face it head on and come out on top."

Director Graves began going over the training plan, but I found myself having trouble concentrating. There was already so much always on my plate trying to meet my parents' expectations. But I was lying to myself if I thought that wouldn't go on the backburner while trying to retrieve the Runner. With an uncertain timeline before the mission, I needed to put my all into every bit of training. Maybe I'd make some changes to Gale and improve its abilities as well. Whatever I could do to hold the line for the actual professionals.

Learning from the Best

We trained inside a GPA facility that resembled our school gym, including a painted track near the perimeter. Any confidence I felt from recognizing equipment in the weight room vanished when the workout started in earnest. My first mistake was assuming *any* of our previous work mattered. Running around town during errands and lifting some weights was nothing in the face of Agent Daniels' basic conditioning. Intermittent sprinting, by his definition, involved long, high-speed bursts followed by recovering with a quick jog. There was no option to walk. If we fell, we pushed ourselves to get back up and match the pace of the next slowest person. Our bodies ached with each step. Fire burned in our lungs as we gasped for air.

But there were no breaks until Agent Daniels allowed it. If ever we began to complain he simply reminded us that Ray had called us superheroes. That was enough to keep the big lug himself going. Eve was driven by her natural competitiveness,

Sarah by her ferocious savior-complex. It was heartening to see the three of them continuously improve. I had no choice but to keep up. The voice of my father berated me whenever I fell behind. I'd already failed him twice. If I couldn't do this, I'd fail not only him, but myself.

Strength training immediately followed the sprints. Agent Daniels measured our abilities before the first session. After that he always gave us goals that seemed unattainable. If we made the mistake of reaching those goals, we got a new one. By the time strengthening ended every evening, we hurt all over. Recovering quickly was also part of being battle ready. Exhaustion and pain were commonplace in a fight. We couldn't allow ourselves to stop from the discomfort. Agent Daniels' recontextualized our challenges to make them easier to face. It was necessary so we could keep going since our daily routine didn't end when physical training did.

After our bodies were broken, we strengthened our minds. Tactical training was handled in a simple meeting room where a large diorama was set up with small figurines representing Oghrodi, GPA agents, and the Glaives. Agent Daniels, with the help of his colleagues, created scenarios for us to work through. There wasn't any sort of right answer, but he made it clear when we made foolish decisions. From random civilians to broken equipment, there was always something getting in the way of our ultimate goal of defending against the Riftwalkers. Roleplaying as the Glaives came easier to the others. Ray was on top of defense and using his bat while Eve was moving in dimensions no one else could. Sarah was thinking of uses for Jade that I couldn't imagine. I often struggled to keep track of what each Glaive was capable of, even Gale. The suggestions I gave, while usually possible, were often ill-advised.

Finally, we each had specialized individual training to finish off the day and fill the weekend. One of the agents trained Ray with a variety of bludgeoning weapons. Meanwhile, Eve was taught how different GPA firearms worked. A rotation of agents trained Sarah in different capture techniques and rescue operations. I, on the other hand, was set up with a glorified training dummy. It stood almost nine feet tall and changed parts every session. In a single room I had to fight at my best for ten minutes at a time. Agent Daniels watched over me, but said nothing to assist. If it ever got too dangerous, the dummy stopped and I was dismissed. Most of the time I was the first one back in our dorm for the night.

The dorm was everyone else's favorite part of our current situation. It had two bedrooms and a decently sized common room. Aside from the nice bathrooms there weren't many other commodities. We were meant to rest there outside of training, and the others found joy and peace. Sarah set up a speaker that played music while everyone unwound. We spent almost all of our very limited free time there. It was great, but I found it almost impossible to relax. I was fixated on improving myself. I didn't want my friends to think I was avoiding them, but I struggled to focus on conversations unrelated to our predicament.

"How can you do that?" I asked Ray while he was reading a comic. "I can't take my mind of training."

"It's a different kind of training." Ray held up the cover, showcasing a muscular superhero clad in primary colors thrusting his fist in the air. "I need to know what kind of superhero *everyone* loves. How do they make people feel safe? Hopeful."

"Probably one who can save everyone."

Ray shook his head. "If there's one thing I've learned from years of comics: No one can save everyone. I created multiple Glaives so if one of us falls short, the others can fill in the gaps."

"It's why we all have different powers," Eve added from her seat across the coffee table. "Ray's been saying something similar since I joined the project."

"What convinced you to give me chains?" Sarah was leaning against the counter, making popcorn.

"Don't you prefer saving people to fighting Riftwalkers?" Eve challenged.

Sarah hummed. "It leaves me a bit lacking in the combat department. I'll figure something out."

I turned to Ray, "What's *your* plan if you fall short?"

"My suit is designed like a tank is so I can mess up, take hits, and keep standing." A cheeky smile stretched across his face. "You guys can solve my problems for me."

Eve smirked. "Not very heroic of you."

"I'm just a regular guy where you three are concerned," Ray said.

"The fact you're ready to fight aliens is pretty irregular, if you ask me," Eve countered.

"Aren't we all?" Sarah asked.

Everyone responded with scattered acknowledgments but I felt like a liar. Knowing the others felt ready for our mission only stressed me out more. The feeling of falling behind weighed heavily on me. In order to catch up I began waking up early to get some extra time with the training dummy. I couldn't use it without Agent Daniels being there so I had to find him. He often bragged about the crazy hours he kept so I assumed he had to be up. Luckily, I stumbled upon him training with heavy bags in the weight room, boxing with a mastery he'd never shown before.

"Are you kidding me?" I blurted out, grabbing his attention.

"Oh. Good morning, Anand. I'm guessing you need me for the dummy." Agent Daniels said.

"I told you— Hell, you've seen me box! Yet you won't just teach me yourself?"

The agent's usual annoyed expression appeared. "No, I won't." He stepped around the heavy bag and leaned on the bar holding it. "Honestly, I wish none of you kids were here. That's why I'm helping you in the first place. You shouldn't be on a battlefield, but if it's gonna happen, I'm making damn sure you're prepared."

"You're doing a shit job of it with me! The others all get personal training, but I'm stuck flailing against a robot while you silently watch. I get stopped early more often than not, but you never tell me why!"

"Consider it a consequence of relying on hand-to-hand combat."

I threw my hands up. "That's rich coming from you."

Agent Daniels shook his head with a deep sigh. For a few moments he said nothing, contemplating his next words. Because he handled our group training, I could only assume he had an issue with me specifically. I had been wondering what I was doing wrong, but it was hard to glean since the only interactions we had outside of training were when he talked to Gale and later recruited me. Maybe the progressive widening of the skill gap between my friends and I was bothering him. But it was his responsibility to help with that!

"Boxing can be great in an unarmed fight against other humans. I still practice, but haven't used it. Specialized weapons are necessary during Oghrodi encounters. *You* don't have something like that beside the suit," Agent Daniels explained. "I won't deny that I find it novel. Your Glaive makes fighting hand-to-hand possible. Not to mention, you don't run the risk of getting disarmed."

"Eve and Sarah have their weapons attached to their suits. They can't be disarmed," I interjected.

"Yes, but their weapons demand a very specific fighting style. Eve prospers at long range and Sarah is good up to mid range. If their gear gets destroyed, they'll fall back on the basics of basic combat training. You won't."

"Ohhh, yeahhhh. I'll fall back on my random flailing," I replied.

"You don't flail. I don't know if you're that unaware of your body, but you move very precisely. Since you can't solely rely on boxing against the big dummy you've begun using your legs." Agent Daniels huffed. "You want the truth? Director Graves wanted me to teach you to box. I declined, but offered to oversee your specialized training anyway."

"So why do you stop me every time I'm about to have a breakthrough? I find an opening to exploit on the dummy and you send me back to the dorms. The next day the dummy's way stronger and I'm back to square one."

"Tell me, Anand. What would you do once you broke past a limit? Beat down the dummy for several minutes and then have to wait for an upgrade anyway. When things get easy, your mind idles. When things are hard, you chase success. There's a deep determination in you to surpass yourself. I want that to be your default state-of-mind. You should never be complacent if you're putting yourself directly in an enemy's range of attack."

My lips flapped silently like a fish gasping for air. Trying to be better everyday was something drilled into me, but I didn't realize that it had made me unfocused when my mind wasn't active. It was true that I'd spent every night here thinking of how to move when fighting the dummy. Looking back, there was no awkward flailing in my attacks. Maybe at first, but they were getting sharper as I tried to break down my opponent. At some point I'd forgotten that I was risking my life every time I engaged the enemy. Training at my upper limit kept me focused at all times. Agent Daniels was right, staying that way during a real fight would be crucial and he had drilled it into me effortlessly. The feeling was ingrained without my notice. If not for him pointing it out, I might have never realized what happened. I didn't know if I was angry or in awe of Agent Daniels mentorship, probably both.

Finally, I muttered, "I still feel like I could punch better."

For the first time ever, Agent Daniels cracked a genuine smile. "Yeah, that's fair. Sometimes a single punch can end a fight. At least a solid one. How about this: What one punch do you want to master?"

"Just one?"

"The basic form of every punch is the same. But the one you master will become part of you. When your back's against the wall, that attack will be all you can do."

"Well, I'm right handed."

Agent Daniels shook his head. "That is barely an answer. Okay, we'll go with a straight." He took a basic boxing stance and threw out his right hand.

I mimicked it to the best of my ability. "I thought this was a cross."

"Same thing. What matters is learning to throw it properly." He walked towards me and pushed my shoulder lightly, knocking me off balance. "We'll start with fixing your stance. That'll help universally. Then the straight so you have a real weapon in your arsenal."

"You think it'll still be good even though I'm fighting monsters?"

"Gale triggers your instincts and strengthens you in ways you might not notice. Your stance gets sturdier. Those treads of yours allow for movement that humans aren't capable of. Even those air thrusters could be used to amplify your attacks." The agent nodded slowly as he ran through the Glaive's abilities. "If you master a straight as you are, Gale's version will be unmatched."

Ever since then, Agent Daniels took a slightly more hands-on approach to my personal training. I had so many questions about boxing but he never humored them. All he would focus on was my form and the basic cross. He never even corrected my jab. My primary focus remained on combatting the training dummy with Agent Daniels oversight. He made sure to constantly remind me, he wasn't there to teach me boxing. Much like the straight punch, he wanted the words to be branded into my mind.

"You're not here to be a boxer. You need to be a fighter."

Reality Check

A meeting for the retrieval operation was scheduled during the end of our third week with the GPA. Unfortunately, we weren't allowed to take part. Training was cancelled which freed us for the day. I decided to spend it practicing, but Ray stopped me before I could leave our room.

"Wanna grab brunch?" he asked.

"I wanted to train—"

"Take a break," Ray said forcefully then switched to his usual levity. "We haven't grabbed a bite, just you and me, in a while."

I put my hands up in surrender. "Okay, I'm taking a shower first, though."

It was rare that Ray's demeanor ever changed so I was sure he needed this chat. The only problem was I had no clue what it could be about. We'd been friends for as long as I could remember, but with that came the knowledge that Ray was unreadable when he was serious. On the other hand, figuring him out was easy as long as he was in happy-go-lucky mode. When I got to the living room, I overheard him whispering with Eve and Sarah about "handling it", but decided not to pry.

Once we got out of the GPA building, we walked in silence towards the Original Pancake House a couple miles away. The mild, late spring weather was difficult to enjoy with the silence between us. For a while Ray simply muttered to himself until he finally calmed down.

"You've been stressed," he said, stride unbroken.

I chuckled a little at the obvious statement. "I mean, yeah. I'm surprised the rest of you aren't."

"We are. But we've been able to stay calm together. You've been facing it alone. Not literally, but like, in your head."

Part of me wanted to deflect, but Ray was taking the longest break we got to talk to me. The least I could do was be real with him.

"For a while I felt like I was falling behind. In a way I feel like I still am." A breath caught in my throat and I had to force it out. "You made the Glaives and are, like, the definition of a superhero. Eve improves them and has so much knowledge to contribute to humanity. Sarah's taken her love of people and become a great protector. Meanwhile, I'm just following along."

"So you're not worried about training..." Ray said.

"Not really. I think I'm doing alright there."

"You think you're doing 'alright?'" Ray chuckled. "I'm not gonna poke that. Why do you feel like you just follow along?"

"I mean, you're the one who always talked about superhero teams," I answered. "I joined Project Glaive because you needed people."

"By that logic just Eve and Sarah would've been enough. Do you really not get why you joined us?"

The question hit close to a part of myself I had trouble accepting. Namely that I had no clue why I did certain things. I guess I always felt like taking the path of least resistance, leaving as much brain power as possible for more important things. Whatever that meant.

"You help people all the time," Ray continued. "Especially the ones you're closest to. I mean, your dad's such an asshole and you're working so hard to get him back."

"I don't know if that's true. I... haven't thought about him once since leaving home." Something broke in me and tears welled in my eyes. "I don't even know if I care about him. Can you believe that? What kind of son doesn't care about his own dad?"

Ray planted his left hand on my shoulder. It was an intentional thing he did when wanting to connect with people. That act alone made my heart jump to my throat.

"If going through your grueling personal training is a sign of you *not* caring; I shudder to think what caring looks like. Seems to me you're trying to measure yourself by Arjun's definition of caring. I don't think anyone can figure that out. But by mine you do nothing but care about him, even when it's to your detriment."

"The training has nothing to do with him," I said while shaking my head furiously. "I need it to keep up. Otherwise I'm just playing pretend in a suit."

"We're *all* people in suits. None of us are *pretending* to be superheroes. This is why I made a point about the difference between Glaives and *Glaives*. Were you not listening?" Of all of Ray's explanations, this one always sounded the most ridiculous. "The *Glaives*, emphasis on the capital G, are superheroes. They give people hope and protect them from monsters. That's only possible because at the end of the day, it's humans in the suits."

I huffed. "I get what you're saying. But I don't have that voice telling me to help people. Gale is the one who's driven to make life better for everyone."

"Are you that stupid?" There was a genuine confusion on Ray's face and frustration in his voice.

He finally stopped walking and I followed suit a few steps away. This time there was no quiet muttering. Instead, he tightly shut his eyes while taking a deep breath. After several long moments, he nodded, opened his eyes and exhaled sharply. He briskly walked past me before speaking and made a point not to look my way.

"Do you remember when I lost my arm?" Before I could answer, he continued. "Sorry, that was a crazy question. I was planning to bring this up during your wedding..." He paused briefly. "Once I healed, most people took my smile at face value. You saw past it and asked if I needed help with things. It was little, we were only eight, but it meant the world to me. Then you stopped asking. Instead, you moved through the world making my life easier without bringing any attention to it." The idea of talking so candidly made me cringe, but Ray was gleaming as he reminisced. "My backpack was always on my left when it was time to leave class. You always walked on my right as if to keep me safe. Hell, you still habitually stand on that side of me. Eventually I noticed you didn't just do it for me or Eve or Sarah. It was everyone you could reach. If someone needed help, you did everything in your power to provide it. *That's* the superhero spirit."

I tried to respond. "But the Glaives—"

"Are suits. And I'm pretty sure my definition for them was wrong since Eve told me actual glaives are basically spears." Ray seemed exasperated remembering a different conversation. "Gale is a codename. That's it. The only time Gale is a person is when *you* become a Glaive. Again, capital G."

"We *always* spell it with a capital G." I challenged lamely.

With every word Ray spoke I had more trouble denying his claims. It was clear he believed what he was saying about me.

Ray took a deep breath. "You're gonna hate me saying it, but Arjun is right about your potential. He's just wrong about what it's for. When I brought you into the team you mentioned that I always say 'the world could use superheroes.' You do realize I got that from you, right? You said it the first time I brought over some manga when we were kids."

"Even if that's true, it doesn't mean I came up with it," I contested.

"Doesn't matter. To me, that phrase matters cuz my best friend believed it. Somewhere inside, not even deep down, you still do. It's my job to make it a reality. In fact, the first Glaive I ever designed was Gale. Because I knew if anyone had the potential to be a superhero, it was you."

"Belief is one thing, but to put in that much work for one person... I couldn't do that," I admitted.

Ray cracked his signature wide smile, "That's why I'm *your* best friend. What you can do, for all our sakes, is just chill out a bit. Keep training, but remember to take a break. Going full force will only burn you out before the mission."

There had been a noticeable difference between how calm the others looked compared to me. Everyone was on top of homework and training, but I looked haggard. My brain was firing on all cylinders unnecessarily. Regardless of what was coming, I had to consider the kind of life I was leading. I'd become a workaholic just like my dad without realizing it. The very idea sent chills down my spine.

As we reached our destination, we changed the conversation. The weekend crowd at Original Pancake House was bustling. We lucked out with two counter seats and ordered our meals. Everyone was engrossed in their food so we could talk, but had to be a bit more vague.

"What exactly did you have in mind for me to relax?" I asked.

"Plenty of things; read some comics, listen to music, join our dance parties, ask out a girl. You know, normal life things." The grin plastered to Ray's face had shifted firmly from friendly to smarmy.

"My parents—"

"You basically have a part time job they'd never agree with. Can't use that excuse anymore."

Even I knew it was weak reasoning. It's not like I hadn't considered it myself. Every passing day around Sarah brought the idea to mind. Especially now that we'd basically lived together for a few weeks. I could probably maintain a romantic relationship as long as I kept my parents a healthy distance away from it. But I never talked about any of these thoughts. It should have been obvious Ray would bring it out of me.

I sighed. "I don't want to make our friendship awkward."

Ray hummed and nodded emphatically. "Have you listened to the Raylist^{TM} recently?"

He said the 'tm' out loud, he always did. It was a playlist he had started several years ago with songs that inspired him. Eventually we all began sharing it, but Ray was always bugging me in particular to listen to it whenever it was updated. At least the choice in songs was good. Plus it kept me from having to look for new music.

"Do you have to say the full name every time?" I asked.

"Yeah. Now answer the question," Ray insisted.

"Uh, a bit. I keep looping the first few songs when I'm training. Why?"

"As you know, Sarah's maintains it almost as much as me. Which is great and I love her taste in music, don't get me wrong. But, she's been getting pretty heavy handed with her recent additions."

Our meals arrived as he pulled out his phone and scrolled to the bottom of the playlist. There were at least ten songs with a very apparent romantic vibe to them. I recognized a few of the titles from the radio, and the ones I didn't made no effort to hide their subject matter.

"It's nice and all, but it ruins the vibe of the Raylist™." Ray didn't even bother trying to hide his smile behind the melodrama. "I think the best option is for you to finally ask her out so she eases up on the message."

"Why would she be doing that now?" I asked.

"Come on, man. That should actually be obvious to you." Ray cut his pancakes while giving me time to respond, but continued when I didn't. "Things have been rough for months now. She thought she'd die during that first anomaly. We're about to do a really scary job. Maybe, just maybe, she'd like something to look forward to on the other side."

"Why not just ask me out herself then?"

"Oh, that's where Eve and I agree. You're both cowards. It's a perfect match."

I grumbled and took a bite out of my eggs benedict. "Do you two just sit around discussing people's love lives?"

"Just yours. We're very invested."

An elderly couple nearby snickered, but quickly quieted down when they saw me look over. I could feel my cheeks burning and noticed Ray laughing too. Clearly Sarah was right about my emotions being plastered on my face. It was nice that she knew me so well. Feeling happy about that only made me more embarrassed.

"I saw the three of you talking before we left," I said. "Does Sarah know you're bringing this up?"

Ray shook his head. "She and Eve just wanted to make sure I had some sort of game plan to get you to chill out."

"And you landed on telling me to ask Sarah out."

"Again, very invested."

Any thoughts I'd had of romance were all but gone since joining the GPA. The only thing on my mind aside from training was death. Specifically the idea that my father might no longer be around and what that would mean. My goals were to make sure that wasn't the case. For some reason I hadn't once considered the fact that I was vulnerable too.

My life so far had been lived for my parents. I felt like I hadn't done a single thing I really cared about aside from joining Ray in his quest to make superheroes a reality. Otherwise I just leaned on Eve for her intelligence and acumen to improve my Glaive. When it came to Sarah, we'd made an art of never pushing past the bounds of friendship.

I expected Ray to say something more, but he just studied my face while eating. Maybe I was the only one who felt awkward in the quiet. I watched him with equal intensity while scarfing down my food. Neither of us gave an inch in the stalemate of silence. It was possible he was actually looking for something in my eyes. All I wanted to do was make him feel as unsettled as I did. Then again, the boy never shied away from anything, least of all sincerity.

The silence between us continued even while he paid for the meal and we walked back. Not until we could see the GPA base did I finally speak.

"After the mission. Once we've saved everyone."

"You'll ask her out?" Ray asked. "Gonna finally live your life a little?"

I couldn't control the sigh that came out. "Bear with the messed up Raylist for now."

"*TM*." A wider grin than any Ray had shown all morning stretched across his face. "I don't actually mind it that much. Added a few of those songs myself. Just rearranged everything to make a point."

I shook my head and chuckled lightly. Ray must have been really worried if he actually put work into this sort of stunt to reduce my stress. Honestly, it was my fault for falling for it. Some part of me probably wanted to. Then again, Sarah hadn't necessarily hidden that she knew how I felt *or* how she felt. I just couldn't respond honestly. It was cowardice to use my parent's expectations as an excuse. And if there was one person in the world who could make me see that for what it was, it was Ray.

Operation Beacon

The rundown of Operation Beacon shared with us coincided with a public broadcast. It was the first time civilians were informed of the GPA and Glaives collaborating. I would've loved to experience the announcement in person, but all essential team members were being moved to Nebraska as it aired. There was always a fear of overzealous people interfering with GPA operations and getting themselves hurt. To avoid that we were flown out the morning of the mission.

The most memorable part of the flight was getting an eagles' eye view of destroyed Nebraska. Muggy clouds of dust hung over the landscape. The state had no distinguishable features except a several hundred foot high wall surrounding it.

"Doing okay?" Ray asked from his seat next to me.

"Yeah, much better."

It'd been a couple days since our talk, but I'd taken my friend's words to heart. I rested more during breaks and had made a point of interacting with everyone in ways unrelated to training.

The nerves were still there, but I wasn't as overwhelmed by them. With a relaxed mind it was possible to see the anxiety everyone else was feeling as well. That awareness made it easier to be there for them as they had been for me. We were as mentally prepared as we could be.

Our group was among the last to arrive. The underground base of Nebraska was accessed via massive elevators hidden in strategic locations within the towering wall. Unfurnished lobbies were connected to other more secure rooms by long tunnels with moving walkways.

The lab we'd be guarding was on the west side of the base with a massive metallic pedestal in the center. It housed a chipped, gray rock; the extracted Oghrodi beacon. Thick cables extended from the pillar to various wall ports, their purpose unknown to me. Along the perimeter of the room, monitors displayed different angles of the planned battlefield. We split up to study the arena while we waited.

Eve caught up to me. "Doing alright?"

"Yeah, don't worry. Thanks again for setting up those last minute codewords."

"No problem. What's your plan with them?" The concern was understandable, considering what I'd asked of her.

"They're to cover for my lack of a weapon," I explained. "In case pure hand-to-hand combat fails."

Eve nodded and exhaled. "Okay. I only did it because it was *you* asking. Ray would have gone nuts with those modifications."

"What about Sarah?"

"She wouldn't ask. If the primary function isn't for saving people she doesn't even think about it."

"Fair."

Something caught her attention and she split off. Finding the sections of the room that would allow me to fight without damaging any equipment was my priority. I figured the special insulation woven into the walls and floor should shield them from Volt's blasts. And they seemed sturdy enough to resist even our most powerful blows. The only risk I could think of was possibly ripping apart the plated cables with Gale's treads. Everything seemed in order as the intercom in the base came on with Director Graves' voice.

We were minutes out from the operation. As the director promised, the Glaives only had to stand guard. Whatever came through the giant rift wasn't our problem unless it came knocking. That seemed unlikely given the amount of work put into the operation. While my friends and I were training, the GPA had upgraded the fabricator. Dozens of cahlium infused weapons had been produced to individual specifications. They didn't require mutation to use so every agent on the surface of Nebraska was armed with new gear. The more I learned about cahlium, the more I was convinced it was magic.

"Hey, focus up. You're okay, right?" Sarah patted my arm.

"Yeah, yeah." I chuckled softly. "Did you all plan to check on me?"

"Just in case."

A few months ago, that might have bothered me, but now I appreciated the sentiment. When she smiled at me I couldn't help, but reciprocate. It was about time I stopped avoiding the crux of my discussion with Ray.

Trying to be as nonchalant as I could, I asked, "By the way, can we talk after this is over? Just you and me, I mean."

"Whoa, whoa. Hold on, buddy. No throwing up death flags," Ray interjected as he and Eve joined us.

"It's not a death flag!"

"Telling someone about your feelings before a dangerous mission is the *definition* of a death flag."

"That's not what I did!" I argued.

"Close enough."

"Shut up, Ray!" Sarah shouted with reddened cheeks. "Eve, please punch your brother *after* the mission."

Eve smiled mischievously. "Happy to."

"Thank you." Sarah then turned to me and said, "I'd love to."

Ray's shenanigans might have eased my nerves, but my blush was as fierce as hers.

"Cool," I replied weakly.

As I completed my final task before Operation Beacon, humming echoed throughout the room and Director Graves gave the order to get ready. Monitors came online and the beacon pedestal began to glow. Small screens on the surface of the pillar displayed information that was beyond my understanding. What mattered is that whatever system it linked to said everything was within parameters. One of the monitors on the walls was dedicated to tracking cahlium levels. With the beacon in the room, it spiked drastically even before the rift opened.

"Glaives, unsheathe," Director Graves requested.

"Hold on." Ray took a deep breath. "On my queue. Ready?"

It was the last unserious thing he could do before embodying the hero, Quake.

We granted Ray's request and replied in unison, "Ready."

To my surprise, Sarah still struck her practiced pose before transforming. I turned to see Ray extend his right fist out and run his left hand along the top from the forearm to the bicep. Even Eve did a spin before crossing her hands across her choker then extending them out. Meanwhile, I awkwardly stood by as we all unsheathed. The energy behind the transformation codeword was different and I understood just a little more what Ray was always spouting on about. While our conversation had eased my tension, it still hadn't convinced me of everything he believed. Once Gale was standing with the other Glaives, there was no Anand to speak of.

While all the GPA agents had weapons, some also had new armor. Specifically captains were given full face helmets that attached to the collar of their combat suits. A plain gray shell and thin visor made them look distinctly less bombastic than Quake's inventions. Once clicked into place, however, they functioned almost identically.

"Don't get antsy kids. The adults will handle this," Agent Daniels said, triggering a white flicker in the corner of the Glaives' HUDs.

Only he and the director could communicate directly with the Glaives. It had taken some begging and GPA oversight for the teenagers to be allowed to keep using their lifelong group chat. In turn, everyone tried to keep it professional, but that didn't last very long.

"Good luck, Agent Daniels," Gale said. "We'll grade you as harshly as you do us."

"Don't get cute with me, brat."

Thanks to the large weapon in his hands, he was easily recognizable in the crowd. Four spiked blades covered the top third of a long metal rod that nearly eclipsed Agent Daniels in height. No doubt such a weapon would wreak havoc in battle.

The hum around the Glaives grew louder then plateaued as the alien beacon hovered over the pedestal. White light shone out so brightly that it made the outer layer appear translucent. Everything shook as the sky was torn apart, manifesting a rift more violently than ever before. An amalgamation of purple and green waves violently twisted within the fracture. While it wasn't a cluster, the single rift was several times larger than anything prior. Over thirty long seconds it widened until it hung a few yards off the ground.

GPA agents waited in stillness on shattered streets surrounded by decrepit buildings. Some hid behind broken walls while others awaited on the flat land. Fingers twitched and grips shifted as they readied for battle.

An ear-piercing screech filled the air as a pair of talons emerged from the portal. A humanoid creature crawled out, netted wings protruding from its back with jagged claws tearing through the skin on its hands. Pincers sprouted from the bottom of its face, covering a mouth lined with jagged teeth. Along its temple, vertical slits opened to reveal an extra pair of grotesque eyes.

"Harpy," Quake muttered.

Several more monsters poured out of the rift, all sporting various mutations. One grabbed Gale's notice as it, solely, appeared incapable of flight. Dust violently kicked up as the winged armada scattered over the GPA agents. Before line of sight completely vanished, several agents began to fight. Agent Daniels threw his weapon at Harpy. It dodged out of the way, but collided with a hammer wielded by a different agent. Liquid concoctions shot from some weapons and slathered the Oghrodi in adhesive. It wasn't enough to stop them, but slowing them down kept vision clear for the grounded humans.

Gale's eyes locked onto a moving shadow within the dust cloud. It appeared briefly as an obscured mass, only to vanish and reappear several hundred feet in a different direction. At first its movements seemed random as it weaved through the battlefield, leaving battered GPA agents in its wake. Their pained screams echoed under the rift, but no one could get them to safety without risking more injuries.

Finally, an alarm sounded through the base.

A panel on the outer wall was torn down by the hulking beast that blitzed through Nebraska. It stood on two legs, only a few inches taller than the Glaives with gargantuan rippling muscles. Its arms had defined blood vessels that pulsated as liquid squirmed through them. Every movement made it seem the creature would burst.

No GPA agents could get to it before it entered the base. Security measures were no match for its incredible strength. Identification scanners mattered little to something that could rip apart doorways. Automated tasers were brushed off with ease. One of the monitors flickered as it bounced between cameras trying to track the Riftwalker.

Quake approached the main door and readied his bat. "It's coming here."

A heavy attack outside landed against the door and dented it.

"So much for impact resistant plating," Volt muttered as she prepared her blasters.

The next hit blew the doors apart to reveal the bipedal creature. Quake hesitated at the plain face that almost resembled a bald human. The unnatural lack of features, tiny dots for eyes and a wide mouth with no lips or teeth felt otherworldly.

"It's so human," Quake stuttered.

"It's not!" Gale said sharply. "Just name it like we usually do. Hell, I'll do it. Beast. There you go."

Quake shook off the stupor. "Wow. You really suck at naming things. But you're right."

"Beacon," Beast growled, its eyes trained on the floating organ.

Each of its slow steps cracked the metal floor. Quake swung at the monster. Muscle shifted rapidly across it's form, shrinking its legs and expanding its arms. The strike made a thunderous sound, but stopped short against Beast's palms. Chains erupted from Jade's arms, twisting around the Oghrodi to bind it in place. Gale rushed in the instant Quake pulled his bat back. The lumbering monster was too slow to stop the cobalt Glaive from getting within reach. He delivered a flurry of blows to its torso, but Beast didn't flinch. It was different from Basilisk, a creature simply too strong to care.

Beast pulled harder at the binding chains, but the links sprouted spikes that dug into its arms. Volt fired a single beam of light directly at the creature's torso. Burns appeared on its muscular chest which Quake targeted with another strike. The attack landed perfectly, but the monster used the chains to keep its footing. They had underestimated the brute's intelligence.

Muscles reconstituted across its form onto its unbound legs. They grew massive while Beast's now slender body slipped free of the trap. With a single jump it soared into the sky, meeting Volt in the air and slapping her to the ground. Thankfully, she was able to soften the impact by activating her jetpack to slow the descent. Quake and Jade rushed to her aid as she crashed to the ground. Once Beast landed on the pillar, it clambered up and found purchase around the translucent containment device. With a guttural scream it slammed its head repeatedly against the casing, blood dripping from its temple. The glass shattered and Beast quickly grabbed the beacon before facing what appeared as a plain wall.

Jade realized first what it was looking at. "Shit, it knows about the emergency ramp. Director, open it up or this place won't last."

The monster barely leapt from its perch before the far wall slid into the ceiling. Behind it, a massive ramp led directly to the surface of Nebraska. Several were installed throughout the base, supposedly quick exits in case of emergency. Unfortunately, they doubled as the perfect escape route for the Oghrodi.

"The rift is closing!" Agent Daniels yelled through the comms.

Gale swore. This setup was only used because they were children. GPA agents were risking their lives on the surface while taking precautions to keep the kids safe. The beacon could have been in a room without an emergency exit to at least slow Beast's escape, but the GPA was too worried about one of the kids dying in an effort to stop the monster.

Volt pushed Quake and Jade away from her. "Enough, the mission isn't over! We trained like mad for this! Even if I get hurt, I'm not gonna die! Not without a fight. That dickhead is charging at our allies. We have to do something."

She flew up the ramp at top speed, a chain latched around her jetpack for Jade to hitch a ride.

"Go for the beacon!" Quake commanded as he leapt after them. Clearly he'd also gotten some upgrades to be able to traverse hundreds of feet in a single bound.

While they all moved first, Gale beat them out of the exit. Beast was already barreling towards the other GPA agents, but there was no way it could outpace the Glaive's superspeed. Unfortunately, he had no idea what to do when he reached the Oghrodi. Its muscles had shifted once again, this time into a thick sleeve that encompassed the beacon.

The distance between the rift and ground grew as it slowly zipped closed. Thoughts of the taken Runner and its inhabitants flooded Gale's mind. Operation Beacon had always been a gamble.

A plan hatched in his mind with such clarity that Gale fully abandoned everything Director Graves and Agent Daniels drilled into him. He had no idea where the others were, but trusted his friends implicitly.

"Back me up," Gale commanded then uttered a codeword he'd requested specifically for a situation like this. "Overdrive."

Dirt shifted as the treads dug in and rapidly spun. Gale's body moved instinctively to compensate for balance. Scattered earth trailed behind the warrior as he reached the rampaging Oghrodi. Beast's tiny pupils expressed shock as it noticed the Glaive that should have been left in the dust.

"Catch me if you can," Gale taunted.

With a controlled power slide, he drifted past the monster and launched towards the portal. Beast reconstituted for mobility, dropping the beacon in the process. One of the captains dove to catch it while others continued fighting. The flying Oghrodi turned their attention to the speeding Glaive. Within seconds they all were gunning for him which left them vulnerable for the GPA to pounce on.

Gale felt the energy from the rift permeating through his body the closer he got. It had a faint pull twisting gravity around it. With every bit of strength he could muster, he leapt towards the rift. Harpy swung at Gale from the right, but he dodged with a controlled air blast from his leg. When another monster tried to assail him, he jumped midair with his other leg's propulsion. Just ahead, monsters encroached from all sides of the portal.

Gale's speed dropped drastically in the air which allowed Beast to catch up with a monstrous jump. It tried to grab Gale while Harpy and its entourage approached as backup. Gale's mind went blank. There was nothing else he could do. None of the codewords could handle this.

"What the hell do you think you're doing?" Jade screamed as a mass of spiked chains wrapped around Beast, stopping it in midair. The question wasn't aimed at the monster.

Volt blasted an electric current from one arm and a searing laser from the other, both tearing into the hulking Oghrodi. "You don't have to do this."

A series of clicks sounded beneath Gale and he saw Agent Daniels' impractical mace. The central rod extended out of the base like a piston and sent the captain skyward. Using the momentum he swung the mass of blades in a wide arc to block several flying monsters.

"God dammit, this is beyond reckless!" he roared.

The gravity of the rift had taken hold of Gale, but it was still slow going. A few monsters remained and if they didn't grab him now they'd join him on the other side.

"Heads up!" Quake bellowed.

A ball of light soared through the sky into Gale's hands. The beacon was no longer a steady white and instead glowed erratically, even giving the Oghrodi pause. Only one person kept moving in the stillness; the crimson superhero wielding his massive bat. Quake got within reach and pressed the blunt end of his weapon against Gale's chest. Without thinking he grabbed the bat with his free hand.

"I'm tearing down your death flag." Quake grunted, pushing Gale through the portal. "Make it back in one piece."

The firm feeling of Quake's bat kept Gale grounded as everything around him went black. Even the beacon no longer produced light in the empty void. A dry laugh escaped unbidden from Gale's mouth. By all metrics, he'd succeeded in his mission to distract Beast.

Aftermath

Monsters crashed down around Quake after he landed. The flying mobs went still when the rift disappeared. Jade and Volt brought Beast to the ground before a GPA agent ended its life. It was hard to watch, but Quake didn't get a chance to process it before Jade slugged him.

"What was that?!" she yelled. "You sent him off on his own!"

"Seriously dude what were you thinking?" Volt asked while holding Jade back. "Did Gale tell you the plan?"

Quake shook his head. "No. But I needed to back him up. Do you really think I could have pulled him out of the rift's gravity?"

Volt sighed. "He was probably too close to retrieve."

"I could have tried!" Jade said. "What good is this thing if I can't save someone with it?"

"You saved dozens of agents by stopping Beast. If you released it to save Gale, other people would be dead. And he might still be lost," Volt argued.

"You might not agree, but it was the best option," Quake insisted. "We don't know where the hell that rift went, but he'll be better off with an extra weapon."

While the portal had closed, the surrounding area was still hectic. GPA agents moved precisely, killing each Oghrodi before they dared move again. Any injured humans were transported to the underground infirmary. The Glaives idled in the chaos.

Agent Daniels joined them. "I take it he didn't tell anyone he was going to do that." He was met with silence and said, "Let's head back for now."

"We're not going back to Wisconsin till Gale is back," Quake insisted.

"I'm saying to get in the base. Don't challenge me on this, kid."

An air of sadness followed the group as they returned to the damaged beacon containment room. Tunnel repairs were happening as fast as possible to allow transit to start again. Stretchers with unconscious agents sailed across the conveyor belts towards well equipped operating rooms. Quake and the others sheathed their suits while trekking along the morose corridors. Loose wiring and broken panels reminded them of the monster that rampaged through the halls. As they got further from the site of the battle, the damage became less apparent. By the time they got to the infirmary it was pristine.

Agent Daniels led the kids to a closed area inside to get checked separately. Somehow, none were completely battered. Even Eve only had a few bruises thanks to Volt's defenses. It impressed and frustrated Ray how well the suits he designed worked. They were the exact reason Anand was dumb enough to jump through a rift! He wasn't supposed to be the reckless one. Since that first rift anomaly in Middleton, he'd been extra stupid.

"You're mumbling," Sarah said dryly.

"I can't help it," Ray grumbled. "It's so stupid."

"What is?"

"Everything!"

"We can use this!" Eve gasped while pulling out her phone. "Anand going through the rift isn't necessarily a bad thing!"

With a firm tone, Agent Daniels said, "Eve, save it."

Ray ran to Eve's side and said, "Wait! Can we still track him?"

"God dammit, enough! You all are to do nothing until I return," Agent Daniels snatched Eve's phone and demanded Ray and Sarah's. "I have to report this."

He exited the infirmary and rushed off to a meeting. Ray, Eve, and Sarah went in the opposite direction to wander silently. They couldn't stay around the injured. In the frenzied halls, after years of waiting, agents craved a chance to study Oghrodi bodies. Full cadavers were available, not just single pieces.

The kids entered a large room, where agents watched an ongoing autopsy. For it to be set up so quickly, it must have been prepped beforehand. Logically, it made no sense to resent them, but Ray found himself fuming at the GPA for moving forward already. The trio grabbed a few chairs in the corner.

Ray slumped into one. "Wasn't the whole point of the mission to save everyone who got kidnapped?"

"Yeah, but the GPA isn't going to call retrieval of multiple Riftwalkers a failure," Sarah replied.

Ever since removing her Glaive, she'd been peculiarly nonchalant about all this. It seemed like she didn't care that Anand was gone. As if he didn't matter since the GPA "won."

Ray blurted out. "What about Anand? Am I the only one who cares about what happened to him? Don't—"

"Stop being stupid!" Eve barked. "Sarah's the one that punched you for helping Anand!"

Ray paused and really looked at Sarah. Tears welled up in her eyes, but she held herself back from crying. She was straight faced with an unfocused, hazy stare. In place of his friend stood a husk. Her usual lively self was gone and Ray had idiotically assumed she was heartless.

"Sorry," Ray said ashamedly.

Sarah shook her head. "We just have to wait for Agent Daniels to figure out the next step."

They sat in silence awaiting any update. Observing an unprecedented Riftwalker autopsy would have been amazing under other circumstances, but none of the kids could focus on it. The person who'd be most excited wasn't there to enjoy it, his absence filled the room.

"It's my fault for helping him," Ray grumbled.

"You were right. If you hadn't he'd be dead," Eve replied.

"For all we know, he is," Sarah said matter-of-factly. The words broke whatever dam had kept her steady and tears rolled down her cheeks.

Eve nodded. "Unless dying was part of Anand's plan, there was no way he'd kick the bucket. You know that."

Sarah was starting to choke up, but she nodded. "But I'm so scared. Is this how…"

"The dread of losing someone is heavy," Eve said softly.

"Yeah. But Anand's learned from everything that happened to our parents." Ray forced a smile. "And don't forget, he's a superhero."

Agent Daniels peered into the room, but didn't enter. He signaled the kids to join him. Something was different about how he moved through the facility. Each forceful step echoed down the hall and people moved out of his way without a word.

"You probably feel a sentiment that the GPA has moved past Anand," he said. "Thankfully, Director Graves isn't so inhumane. She believes we may be able to find a way to open rifts using the Oghrodi we gathered."

"That's why they're already being dissected," Eve realized.

"The lab rats are obsessing over every little thing since it's the first time they can conduct this sort of research. They won't allow us to rush the process. But I'll be damned if we don't save the kidnapped civilians." Agent Daniels' fists were clenched tight. "Director Graves agrees with me. However, on the record, she's against us pursuing the mission right now. Even if we have an inside man."

"So the GPA isn't going to do anything," Sarah muttered.

"No, but *we* are."

They entered a space similar to the Madison GPA fabricator room. There was no alien printer, but a powerful computer connected to at least a dozen screens. Data raced across about the Glaives and Ray recognized some of his friends' notes. Maps across the world tracked different signals, but none were the signature Eve programmed for the suits.

"We've received off the record permission to continue the mission." Agent Daniels explained. "It's just us until we can reach Anand. Once we can work out a plan with him, all other GPA resources are open to us."

"You sound so sure that he's alive," Ray said.

"I'm not. But if there was any doubt about his status, I'm sure you three would've said something. Do you believe Anand is alive?"

Ray answered immediately, "No doubt."

"Definitely," Eve agreed.

Tears still marked Sarah's face, but a familiar steely resolve slowly returned. "He'd better be, so I can kill him myself."

"Then I have no reason to question it." Agent Daniels handed back their phones then turned to Eve. "I kept the tracker going. How's it look?"

"Weird," she replied. "The signal keeps dropping."

Ray hummed. "Our Scabbards have never done that."

"I'm guessing it either has to do with damage to Anand's equipment or because we don't have a proper connection to the rift's destination," Agent Daniels deduced.

His hands danced across the keyboard as he moved between shifting screens. Reports and measurements overlayed different regions of Earth. Triangulation algorithms calculated at rapid speeds while stretching over the planet.

"We've been working on establishing a connection to the other end of the rift for a while," Agent Daniels explained. "If this works, we should be able to contact Anand."

Eve grumbled, "That's assuming going through a rift didn't damage his communication functions."

"Not to mention he's still in danger on the other side," Sarah added.

Ray clapped his hands loudly and stepped towards the screens. "No use twiddling our thumbs. Let's find that idiot."

Unknown Territory

Gale always assumed the inside of a rift would match the outside; a constantly swirling purple wave. Instead, he saw nothing; a void, not the glowing orb or bright red weapon in his hands. Their presence would've been forgotten if not for the death grip Gale had on them. The atmosphere shifted abruptly as he crashed into a pile of metal. It sent a jolt through his body that loosened his grasp. The beacon shattered on impact, but the bat remained intact. It did, however, land with a heavy crash that dented the metal floor. By some miracle the Glaive himself remained undamaged. Credit to Gale's friends for protecting him, even here.

Remembering their anger, a wave of guilt washed over him. But it was too late to go back on his stunt. Gale was the only one who hadn't sustained damage during Operation Beacon. If anyone was going to traverse a rift and search for the kidnappees, he was the best choice.

"Hello?" he whispered into his comm. "It's Gale. Can anyone hear me?"

No response. Of course not. Just because the mapping function was working didn't mean communication would. Gale was on his own for real this time. A steady pounding started in his chest as panic encroached on his frazzled mind. He tried to focus and make a plan. There might not be a way *out* of this situation, but there had to be a way forward within it.

First priority was figuring out where the hell he was. Gale slowly rose to his feet and looked towards the ceiling where the rift had opened. It sent him plummeting into a mess of scrap metal that cushioned his fall. He was at the far wall of a massive room, larger than the beacon containment room of the Nebraska GPA base. Walls stood four stories high with maps and diagrams covering every space. The room was populated by dozens of strange-looking spheres floating at eye level above metal pedestals. One of the walls had a circular door and a control panel to the right of it. There weren't any other visible points of entry. Nothing in here resembled a machine for creating rifts. The erratic beacon must have changed landing locations. As long as Gale kept an eye on the door, he wouldn't be caught unaware. Then he remembered the crimson bat resting in a divot of its own making and the loud crash with which it landed.

Gale dove behind one of the pedestals and held his breath. Soft metallic scrapes emitted from aged plaques and pillars. The squeak of rubber-soled shoes passed through the outside hall, but nothing approached the door.

Several minutes passed.

Gale accepted it was just the sounds of the building. He was safe, or at least as safe as one could hope to be this far behind enemy lines.

He walked to the crater holding Quake's comically large bat. The larger Glaive had no issue lifting it but Gale needed a firm two-handed grip to wield the weapon. Once the bat was secure, he took slow methodical steps through the room.

The spheres floating over pedestals were much like the one in Operation Beacon. Illegible plaques adorned each one. A familiar sensation nagged at the back of Gale's head, the feeling he got whenever reading fabricator screens. Unfortunately, he had never been able to parse the longer strings of symbols.

Gale continued his investigation until he reached a sphere that was apparently in the middle of construction. Familiar shapes engraved on it made clear that it was Earth. Hundreds of animal heads decorated the nearest wall, some Gale had only ever read about; exotic beasts, and long-extinct mega-fauna. Next to the trophies were images of cities in shambles from rift anomalies over the last 23 years.

Gale couldn't piece together the Oghrodi's motivation. But sitting around deciphering them wasn't an option. He'd stayed in one place too long already. One last check of his suit was all he needed to convince himself to continue the mission. There was no time to waste while prisoners awaited saving. At least, he hoped they were alive to be saved. And that they were somehow in this very facility, he didn't like his chances trying to navigate the void beyond. Gale stopped the rising doubts and approached the door.

With a minor force of will, he gave a command to his Glaive, and it vibrated to update the map in his HUD. He was in an offshoot room in the middle of a seemingly random hallway. The same instincts that helped him save people on Earth warned that there was danger now in certain directions. Going left out of here wasn't possible with his body screaming to be wary. He decided to go whichever way didn't trigger his fight or flight response. Pressing his hand on the control panel, the door opened with a faint hum and he crept out.

Though the Oghrodi tracked humans with vibrations like the Glaives, it was still good to try and stay hidden. Shadows washed over the metallic blue suit, letting it blend into the gray walls all over the building. At times the light would catch on the bright metal highlights of the suit, just for an instant, as Gale dashed from one piece of cover to another. Those instants were terrifying, but Gale kept his cool. He planned each movement meticulously before following through. All that combat and tactical training was beginning to pay off.

Navigating the empty halls reminded him of walking through school in the middle of class. Of course, Middleton High didn't have towering ceilings and walls made of alien metal. There was a non-zero chance it was cahlium. Much like in the trophy room, every door had a small control panel next to it.

Gale avoided touching them, but recognized some of the text. It wasn't Oghrodi script, it was human, though he didn't notice any languages he had a chance of understanding. Gale would have studied it more, but heard familiar whispers in the distance. He walked slowly towards them and was able to discern the words; the familiar annoyance of a tired worker.

"I think we can be smarter about this," a voice said.

Gale continued down the hall and rounded a corner before approaching a large doorway. Someone waited inside. Gale's instincts screamed for him to be careful. He'd only heard Oghrodi use single words and they were always stilted and awkward. This voice had to be human.

"Yeah, I know. But this is ridiculous," it complained. "Hold on, someone is coming. I will report back."

Gale placed a hand on the panel and slipped through the door. Regret immediately washed over him as he saw a creature that stood eight feet tall. It had faded blue skin and gray eyes. Long hair fell down to its back and partially covered the creature's metallic armor. Each hand had four fingers donned with intricate bladed rings. Behind it was another barred door that it was clearly guarding. Gale filed it away in his head as "Witch."

The creature tilted its head, furrowed a brow, and growled, "What are you?"

Gale swore under his breath and got in an awkward fighting stance. Wielding the massive club forced an unfamiliar pose. Still, it was good enough to defend with. The Oghrodi leapt forward and clawed at Gale's head. He stepped back to make space, but slammed into the door. It had shut automatically. The tiny room was suffocating.

Witch slammed a fist against the wall near Gale's head. He weaved to the side before slipping into reach of the creature. Mustering all his strength, he swung his leg into the Oghrodi's rib. Intense practice with Agent Daniels had drilled proper form into Gale. The attack would be powerful as long as he was stable. It was hard not to be with the massive counter weight on his other side. The strike tore into Witch's armor, forcing it back. The creature's face showed more surprise than pain. Gale spun and swung the weighty bat, only for the monster to backstep. With Gale completely open, the monster leapt forward and swiped its claws across his chest. The Glaive barely dodged, colliding with the wall. Deep cuts marked the front of his chestpiece.

"Foolish," Witch taunted.

It dug all its claws into the wall on either side of Gale. Metal scratched against metal, its blades cutting through the barricade. Witch strained to clap its hands together in an attempt to slice Gale between them.

His heart raced as the blades closed in. Gale moved instinctively. One foot planted against the wall. Treads began to spin and sent him skyward. The claws were too slow to catch the rocketing Glaive. He leapt off near the ceiling and landed behind the monster. Pivoting, Gale swung the bat through his opponent's legs. A grotesque crack echoed in the room followed by a series of squelches. The lower half of Witch shattered, bones and muscles ravaged. Orange blood sprayed across Gale's armor and pooled on the floor. The Oghrodi fell to the ground, but still held up its arms in a fighting stance. No matter how much venom was in its eyes, the fear was evident.

"Surrender," Gale commanded with the bat raised.

When the creature tried to scream he rammed the blunt end of the weapon into its chest. It slammed against the wall and slumped over, coral ichor clinging to its form. Gale prayed he hadn't crossed a line. He stepped closer to check and noticed the unconscious creature faintly breathing.

There was more blood than Gale had ever seen before. He backed away on shaky knees, slamming the bat into the ground for support. The adrenaline quickly washed away and he rested his head on the hilt. The boy inside the suit cowered at his handiwork. This was more visceral than anything he'd ever done before. He was thankful to have not resorted to killing.

Upon further examination of the room, it was much larger than Gale had realized. The pool of blood had felt massive, but it only covered a small portion of the room. The guarded door was adjacent to a panel with a scanner. Surprisingly, it accepted Gale's hand. It occurred to him that the Glaives and Oghrodi had much in common, but now wasn't the time to ponder that. After retrieving Quake's bat he stepped into the next room.

A familiar wind brushed past him under the blue sky that hung miles overhead.

"What the—?"

Massive buildings encircled a cul-de-sac surrounded by a park which led to a sandy desert. Clear skies and sunlight stretched endlessly past the residential area. Gale reached down to touch the sand and felt a cold metal floor. The image of grains distorted around his hand. He looked back to the sky and, after a minute of constant focus, realized the clouds never changed. Whenever they flew to a certain point, they looped back to the other side of the sky with no new formations ever appearing. Everything was *too* perfect. Even the sun never shone down unpleasantly; always hidden from view. Perplexed, Gale approached one of the possibly fake buildings; a simple, undamaged apartment complex. Once he was close, someone shouted from around the corner.

"Now!"

Gale pivoted. Something obscured his vision and draped around his head. From how many fists and feet were hitting the Glaive, there was definitely more than one person attacking. Fortunately, none of them really hurt at all. They bound his arms and legs before dragging him across the floor. A tight knot of thick rope tied him to a metal pole, possibly a faux streetlight.

"Don't stop!" someone commanded. "Show it we won't stay here quietly!"

Another voice. "Let's kill it and take the keys to get out of here!"

"Wait!" a third voice yelled. "I recognize it. It was on the news."

People murmured, but did as the commanding voice ordered. The binding loosened, Gale was pulled to his feet, and the sack off of his head. Exhausted humans looked fearfully at the blood-soaked metal warrior. He scanned the crowd, searching for words to ease their minds. Any he'd mustered vanished when he made eye contact with the contemptuous man known as Arjun Desai.

He saw the Glaive looking over and said, "You are one of the heroes from the news."

"Superhero," Gale replied involuntarily. He definitely couldn't match Quake's gusto, but being shy here would only make the civilians panic. "My name is Gale. I am here to rescue you."

"A one-man operation?" Arjun asked.

"My team and I got separated." Years of lying to his father made it second nature and the perfect tool for this job. "Unfortunately, my comms are nonfunctional. I'm roaming blindly but... I promise to get you back to Earth."

An unfamiliar smile appeared on the older man's face as he approached. "I am Arjun Desai. I'm impressed by what you and your team have done. Is there any way we can help you?"

Seeing any kindness in Arjun's eyes threw Gale for a loop. Every bit of training went out the window. All the practiced conversations he'd theorized about vanished from his mind. A flash of anger slammed into the pit of Gale's gut. It was unfair that his father could ever be so kind. But it was likely because

Gale had a status worth respecting. Oddly enough, the familiar annoyance brought the warrior back to his senses.

"I'm trying to connect to the systems in here." Gale gestured to the space around him. "Got any ideas?"

"You need to connect to the Oghrodi's network and control system," another familiar man said. Mizzek stepped out of the crowd carrying a small tablet. Somehow they still looked pretty normal. Less haggard than everyone else.

"Do you have any clues about how, Mike?" Arjun asked.

Gale felt sick. Arjun constantly complained about the Rift Report website, yet here he was showing trust and friendship he wouldn't offer his son. Sure he got Mizzek's name wrong, but the feeling behind the comradery bothered the boy. What good was Arjun's trust if it went to everyone else, but his family? But now wasn't the time to be dealing with that. Nearly two hundred people were in need of rescuing.

"Indeed. Gale is not tracking in the system," Mizzek replied.

Gale nodded at the tablet. "How did you get that?"

"We got this off one of the more incompetent guards. I have been able to navigate it and led the plan to break out and free ourselves. We face a problem in that there are no longer any prisoners who can work as a frontline. The GPA agents who came with us were put to death."

Gale's heart sank, but fear had to stay out of his voice. "We don't necessarily need a frontline. What can you tell me about the guard rotation?"

"The guards rotate every hour," Arjun replied. "They have not done any kind of reporting within our earshot so I can only assume they work on that hourly schedule."

"How are you understanding them?"

"Mike translates for us."

Gale grunted affirmatively then lied. "So, we have a little under an hour to find my team and get everyone out of here. *Wonderful*." He ran a hand over his helmet. "First things first, this isn't a Runner's worth of people. Where are they?"

"The cages are within these apartment complexes," Arjun answered, gesturing to the cluster of buildings.

"Any ideas on how to release them? We're not leaving anyone behind."

Arjun nodded. "You would need to get to the control room. Mike has the coordinates on that tablet."

"This tool has all the necessary data to get you to your destination," Mizzek said.

"I'll need you to come with me, if you're up to it," Gale replied. "That thing has too much information not to have bypasses for the locks. I can handle any fights that might come our way though."

"What kind of superhero risks a civilian's life?" Arjun stepped between Gale and Mizzek. "If you must take someone, take me."

It took every fiber of Gale's being not to call his father useless. Not to mention how readily he stepped in for someone else when he'd never backed his own son. He'd risk his own life without considering what it would do to Priti.

"Look, Mr. Desai. Miz—" Gale quickly corrected himself. "*Mike* here clearly has a better handle on what's going on in this place than any of you. However, all these folks seem to be listening to you. They are scared and need a leader. Please take care of them."

"We're not scared!" someone nearby yelled.

"You literally just attacked me and were about to kill me. Seems to me like you were scared," Gale replied before addressing the rest of the crowd. "Listen to me, get everyone ready. We'll create a rift home right here."

"What about the Riftwalkers? Won't they follow?" another voice piped up.

"My team and I will stop them. You all worry about getting through the rift," Gale instructed.

Arjun raised his hand. "What about—?"

"The longer I spend explaining to you, the less time we have to get out of here. Please, just hide and wait for our signal," Gale demanded.

Arjun hesitated and nodded. The group parted so Gale could retrieve Quake's bat before heading to the edge of the "city." With a powerful swing he plunged it into the ground and instructed them he'd be back for it. A fire of hope lit in the eyes of every civilian as they looked upon the massive totem. Ray would definitely need to hear about this.

Mutual Benefits

Gale groaned loudly when he arrived back at the entrance of the prison. There was no obvious panel near the door. Thankfully Mizzek had watched the guards intently and pointed out a faint indent on the wall. With a push of Gale's hand, the hidden panel receded and activated the exit.

Mizzek's eyes darkened upon seeing the unconscious Oghrodi laying in orange ooze. The liquid rippled with each soft breath Witch let out. Gale still felt uneasy near the carnage but Mizzek approached with ease.

"You could not do what was necessary," they grumbled, staring down at the bloody heap.

There wasn't a chance to answer before Mizzek lifted Witch's hand and twisted it back. The Oghrodi's bladed rings plunged into its skull, blood gushing out in a torrent as its life was ended.

"What the hell?!" Gale yelled and pulled Mizzek away.

"You have not dealt with what us prisoners have. I will not apologize for killing this monster," they said.

It felt insane to be so cold about it, but Gale had no right to challenge Mizzek after they'd been kidnapped.

He released them and mumbled, "Let's just go."

The tablet had a detailed map with an obvious path back to the trophy room. It seemed more like a tiny closet compared to other sections. Small green dots moved all around the screen with one remaining still in the room Mizzek pointed at, their present location.

"The green dots are Oghrodi, huh?" Gale muttered.

"Yes. We need to get here." Mizzek pointed to a large room a few corridors away. "We passed the control room when we were moved here." He hesitated as he examined the map. "The other Glaives are not here, are they?"

Gale continued as if the question hadn't been asked. "Most of the Oghrodi are patrolling over there. We should be able to get in the control room and do our jobs easily."

Mizzek nodded. "I will make sure we avoid any cameras."

"As per usual."

It took some work to get the blood cleaned off the main entrance's control panel. A loud grinding sound came from the damaged wall as the door slid open. It wasn't too much of a worry since there were no patrols nearby. Gale took the lead and stuck to the shadows with Mizzek close behind. When another green dot looked like it was approaching them on the map, the duo detoured. Even if Gale could fight them there was no telling when he'd be outnumbered.

"So, how'd Mizzek turn into Mike?" Gale asked quietly after another avoidance.

"I was named Mizzek by my parents. It is customary to shorten your name for those who have trouble with it. Thus your father, and others, know me as Mike." Mizzek didn't bother lowering their volume since the tablet indicated no one else in earshot. "Surely you had a nickname at some point."

Gale hesitated for a second. "Andy. I hated it."

"How did you convince others to use your full name?"

"I couldn't."

"What did you do?"

"If someone wasn't willing to try with my name, I stopped trying to engage with them. Not worth the trouble..."

Gale's voice trailed off when they reached a massive window at the end of an empty hallway. A beautiful, shimmering marble hung in the sky amongst shining specks on an endless black canvas. Slow swatches of white moved along serene blues and greens on its surface. Gale was speechless seeing his home from an angle he had only ever imagined. In the distance was the familiar sight of the lunar marvel that blessed night skies.

"I thought we were further out. On a different planet or something," Gale said.

"I consider a ship in space quite far," Mizzek replied. "Come. We are close to our destination."

The mesmerizing sight was difficult to pull away from, but Gale's constant internal nagging convinced him to move on. In the middle of the next hall was the entrance to the control room. According to the tablet, no one was inside.

This panel didn't have a simple scanner to gain access. Mizzek fiddled with their handheld device and produced two wires from its side that connected directly to the control panel. With rapid movements, they navigated the system and forced the door open. Gale rushed inside, ready for a fight. Thankfully, they were the room's only occupants.

The room was dimly lit with massive cables intricately weaving throughout. Unlike the GPA's thick, messy wires, these ones were integrated perfectly into every surface. A large switchboard was in the center of the room with a hollow upside-down dome and small monitor at one side of it. The opposite side held a large monitor but no visible controls.

"Looks clear. Mizzek, can you interface the tablet and that... thing?" Gale asked. "We need to figure out how to release everyone and get a rift created in the prison."

"Why not release the civilians then lead them to the escape pods?" Mizzek pointed to a separate room on the ship with few guards. "Why create a rift?"

"They'd have to cross this whole ship for a *chance* at escape instead of the guarantee with a rift. Enough of us have gone through one so we know it's safe. There's no reason to avoid it."

"I see."

Mizzek placed the tablet down and started typing on the large monitor without a word. They deftly worked the incomprehensible system, unplugging and replugging wires in the switchboard before returning to the screen. There was no hesitation despite the overwhelming flow of information. Gale just focused on guarding the door, but had a gut feeling no one would attack.

The dome of the system emitted a soft glow before a holographic sphere appeared over it. Features slowly manifested until it was possible to recognize the continents of Earth. The panel underneath lit up with a series of symbols and numbers. While Gale recognized them to be coordinates, he couldn't deduce where they led.

"Opening the cages will trigger an alarm. Creating a rift will do the same," Mizzek explained. "I'm not entirely sure where this rift will send everyone either. What do you want to do, Gale?"

Flashing dots across the Earth represented past Oghrodi attacks. Blindly guessing coordinates for a rift could lead to catastrophic failure. A look of concern passed between the duo as they stood over the rift creation system. There was no way Gale could figure it out when the much simpler fabricator escaped him.

While he was racking his brain for a plan, static buzzed in his headset. Relief washed over Gale as a message rang in his ears. Few things were as familiar or as comforting as his best friend's voice.

"Buddy?"

"Ra— Quake!" Gale was much louder than he intended.

"You idiot!" Sarah cried. "We've been trying to reach you for nearly an hour!"

Eve piped up. "You owe me so many brunches when you get back."

"Why the hell would you do something so reckless?" Ray asked.

"You literally gave me a push," Gale replied in confusion.

Ray groaned. "Because you were too far gone!"

"Oh."

"Is that the other Glaives?" Mizzek asked while continuing to work.

"Yeah," Gale replied. "Did you do something?"

"I patched your suit into the system so it is recognized as an Oghrodi."

Gale's mind raced with questions. First of all, how? Secondly, why would Mizzek even think to try that? Also, had they attached something to the suit to do it? It was torture pushing aside all the questions, but now was not the time to get derailed.

"Uh, I'm kinda patched into the Oghrodi system. Mizzek's here. But they're not connected to the comms," Gale answered.

"How'd they do that?" Eve's obvious suspicion only furthered Gale's.

"Honestly, I have no clue. And we're kind of stuck on what to do next. Apparently an alarm will sound when we release the prisoners and another will go off when we make a rift. Not to mention I have no idea where to aim it"

"Why not head back to the prisoners then free them and open the rift at the same time?" Ray asked.

"That would leave Mizzek alone," Gale answered.

Ray groaned. "It wouldn't be an issue. You know that right?"

"So, I'm not the only one weirded out by them," Sarah hummed. "Good to know."

Eve chimed in with, "Maybe we should've discussed how we felt about Mizzek a bit more openly. Now's definitely not the time for it."

Gale grunted in agreement, but didn't change his demeanor. For the entire team to be on the same page meant he could act on his hunches. But it had to be handled delicately. Just because Mizzek was suspicious didn't mean they couldn't be trusted.

"Volt, can you provide the exact coordinates of where you are? Preferably somewhere wide open," Gale said.

Eve hummed while searching for the information. "Nebraska's surface is our best bet. Ready for the numbers?"

Rather than repeating the numbers out loud, Gale input them into the small panel himself. With each new entry, the sphere rotated and glowed. Sometimes a red line would appear or when two lines met, a dot. The sphere continued to zoom until it hovered over the central part of North America.

"Alright, I'm going to disconnect for a minute. Quake, moderate the chat server," Gale instructed. He turned off his voice comms and approached Mizzek. "How much longer are you willing to help us?"

"What do you mean, Gale?" Mizzek asked.

Even knowing his face was hidden, Gale couldn't help, but stare daggers at Mizzek. "You don't think I'm that stupid, do you? You always refer to me and the others as 'your kind.' You know what Riftwalkers are actually called. Even Ray and Eve don't outright understand the fabricator, but you're navigating the systems here with no problem. You have far too much knowledge about this place for a human. And let's not forget your reaction to the Oghrodi I—"

"—failed to kill. I was simply remedying an unfortunate situation."

"No, you acted psychotic! Plus, you're still not explaining how you understand this stuff. The only way you could do that is if you're one of them!" Gale got in a fighting stance. "What are you?"

Mizzek turned towards the Glaive. "Can we not continue to pretend I am human and work together?"

"I don't trust you." Gale approached warily. "I want to, but I *can't*."

There was a brief silence as Mizzek took their hands off the control system. Tired eyes studied Gale in confusion and pondered something.

"You are correct that I am an Oghrodi," they admitted. "However, I will continue to assist you because I have a vested interest in making sure you succeed in retrieving the humans on this ship."

"So you're some sort of intergalactic altruist?"

"Not in the slightest. Keeping the prisoners hinders *my* goals."

Mizzek's entire body rippled before turning into a woman that would blend into any crowd. There were no telltale signs that the being was an Oghrodi. Their eyes, skin, and hair were all characteristically human.

"I have had time to study and live amongst your kind," Mizzek explained. "Unlike other Oghrodi, I have honed my capability to transform to the point I can mimic your kind perfectly. Do you want to know why? It is rather interesting."

Gale felt sick to his stomach voicing this idea. "We're the same. At some level."

Mizzek transformed back to their most familiar form while clapping. "You always were the smartest of your childish group. Oghrodi are simply evolved versions of humans. It is why those of you who have interacted with our blood can understand my less intelligent allies to some extent. I would be unsurprised if you can translate more of their words as you continue to utilize the Glaives."

Gale didn't dare say anything to confirm the suggestion, but Witch's words haunted his memory. It was the first time he'd understood more than a single word at a time. He'd even mistaken the Oghrodi's voice as human. It was important to know that these changes would happen to every Glaive. He'd need to make sure they were aware.

"There is no reason for you and I to fight. We can help each other. After all, you want those innocent humans to return home," Mizzek suggested.

Gale's mind was racing to figure out the Oghrodi's motive. Ray and Eve were the first people to ever be contacted directly by the Rift Reporter. None of their biggest fans so much as chatted with them. Mizzek came out of hiding to work directly with a group of teenagers. It was never about Gale fighting back Wendigo or his past interest in the Rift Report. For all intents and purposes, it was a coincidence that he was involved in the thing that grabbed the reporter's attention.

"You want the Glaives," Gale said.

Mizzek clicked their tongue. "Always the smartest."

"But why? You can fight us on equal footing."

"Equal footing..." Mizzek spat and their expression darkened. "You vermin have utilized cells from our species to rapidly create a defense against our conquest. Yet the leadership of my armada sees no problem with it! They are antiquated fools who must be shown the danger you pose. Even if you successfully get every prisoner off this ship, I doubt you will all survive. So I have graciously decided to assist you as you complete your last mission."

For the first time, Gale saw a resemblance between Mizzek and Arjun. Both were so sure of themselves that they couldn't perceive anyone beneath them succeeding. It was infuriating. Working within these parameters might be a gamble, but that didn't make it impossible to come out on top. Gale connected to the voice comms before saying anything.

"Alright. I'm going to head back to the prison." His friends gave scattered acknowledgements, but Gale continued as to not draw suspicion. "Once I get there, you'll release the prisoners and open the rift at the same time. At least then I'll have some back up against the Oghrodi that show up."

Mizzek smiled, returning to their post at the control system. "I am glad we can work together and will try to keep Oghrodi numbers to a minimum."

"Whatever." Gale grumbled while walking away.

"How will I communicate with you?" Mizzek asked.

"You can hear me through the surveillance in the prison. I'm guessing there's an intercom you can speak through."

"What if I get attacked? What about *my* safety?"

Gale replied dryly, "You'll be fine."

"Aw, *Andy*, I thought we had bonded."

Gale turned on his heel and spat. "Never call me that! If this gets you killed, that's no sweat off my back. You're the one who was adamant that Oghrodi aren't worth mercy."

Mizzek held up their hands in faux surrender. "Well, you should hurry. There are ten minutes before the guards are supposed to change. Hurry along or a patrol might reach the prison before you. I will keep the path clear so you can return without sneaking around like a rat."

Unfortunately, Mizzek was right. There was no telling if the data shared on the map was even real. Dawdling invited danger. With a single utterance of "overdrive," Gale blitzed away from his former ally.

"Quake, Volt, and Jade, stay on the surface," Gale muttered into the comms, the whirring of his treads doing a wonderful job of hiding his soft voice. "There will be a rift opening within ten minutes. Come through and be ready for a fight. We're getting the prisoners out of here."

"Should we bring more back up?" Ray asked.

"No. Mizzek is only after us. We can't put more people in danger. Think of it as a superhero's duty."

"Roger," Eve said.

"We'll be there," Sarah added.

Ray remained quiet, but Gale could almost hear his muscles tighten in anticipation. He was raring to go.

Back at the prison entrance, the double doorway slid open, revealing the alien corpse. Oghrodi lived without consideration for those they deemed weak. If this plan failed, there was no telling what horrors they would bring down on the prisoners.

Gale rushed through the second door and found Quake's bat undisturbed in the empty cul-de-sac.

"Anyone there?" Gale yelled openly. There was no longer a need for privacy.

From behind the buildings, people slowly emerged. There were far fewer than earlier and his father wasn't among them.

"Where are the others? Are they with Mr. Desai?" he asked.

Someone answered from among the crowd, "Yeah, we split up to get everyone ready to escape."

"What did you tell them?"

"Be ready for an obvious signal. Not to be alarmed if their cage opened and to run for it."

As they chatted, more prisoners joined, including Gale's father.

"Our side of the plan went without a hitch," Arjun explained then paused. "Where is your team? Where is Mike?"

Gale was thankful that his father's presence made lying easier. "Don't worry, my team will be here soon. Mike is handling the control system. I'll make sure they get back to Earth."

Mizzek's voice boomed throughout the room. "Do not be illogical! If you tell them that, they will wait for me. That is what humans foolishly do every time a situation like this arises."

"Glad to know that you can hear this room." Gale sighed.

"What is he talking about?" Arjun asked.

The Oghrodi impostor laughed mockingly. "I am not one of you! Did you not catch on to that sooner? What kind of person interacts with aliens without batting an eye?"

"My son does this kind of thing," Arjun replied meekly, color vanishing from his face. The only reason he didn't fall was thanks to Gale holding him up.

The Glaive spoke softly, "Don't worry about it."

"I-I trusted a monster," Arjun stuttered. "What if they trick us again?"

"Trust me! They won't do anything to harm you."

"You have my word," Mizzek confirmed. "Follow the plan and you will get home safe."

Truthfully, Gale didn't trust the Oghrodi either, but spreading panic was ill-advised. The crowd murmured in fear as they looked to the Glaive for assurance. Both Gale *and* Mizzek wanted the prisoners to escape. As long as that happened, everything was fine.

"Stay calm, everyone!" Gale commanded with his best superhero impression. "Nothing has changed! This escape plan wouldn't be possible without Mike! They are helping you get home. Focus on that!" Before anyone could let doubt cloud their judgment, Gale looked up and yelled, "Rift and prison locks, now!"

Mizzek's voice was drowned out by loud clicking from over a hundred locks. People poured out of buildings in droves. An alarm blared through the room. No doubt it spread throughout the ship.

"Here comes the rift," Mizzek sang over the siren before a massive glowing portal manifested in the prison.

The steady semicircular shape rested calmly on the ground. Some humans approached it before being held back by others.

"What's wrong? Run!" Gale yelled.

"How do we know that will take us back to Earth?" Arjun asked. "This could be a trap."

Gale would test the rift himself, but didn't dare take his eyes off the prison entrance. The doors slowly slid open and Gale readied for a fight. What came through made his blood boil.

The slinky white demon Wendigo had been healed and its long claws modified into thin blades. Next to it, Basilisk, now equipped with a large metal flail in place of its bisected tail. Golem had forgone its flesh and matted fur for stone modifications. Jagged rocks replaced claws and sharp crystals covered the opalescent tentacles.

Mizzek cackled. "Think of this as your opportunity for a retake exam."

Make It Out Alive

Golem's elongated legs allowed it to approach quickly. Its twisted tentacle arms stretched towards the prisoners. Simultaneously, Basilisk skated forward on ooze pouring from its legs. Transparent slime coated the ground as it traveled. The final Oghrodi, Wendigo, had no special tricks. Its claws simply dug into the ground as it clambered monstrously towards the buildings.

Gale moved to intercept when something beat him to it. A black metal bludgeon flew out of the rift and collided with Golem's arms followed by several blasts of light that electrocuted the area around Basilisk. Chains erupted from the rift, grabbing both metal bats and flinging them skyward. A familiar red Glaive burst from the portal and snatched both weapons out of the air. Yellow and green Glaives followed behind with their weapons drawn. Between the civilians and the monsters landed Quake, Volt, and Jade, stunning all of them to stillness.

"Looks like it came in handy," Quake examined his bat covered in dry orange blood.

"Yeah. But it doesn't suit me," Gale replied, joining his friends.

"Who cares? Focus on the mission," Volt commanded, then turned to the crowd. "The rift has proven operational. Go! The GPA is awaiting you on the other side."

Jade yelled out. "If anyone needs help moving, shout now and we will assist you."

She used her chains to lightly pick up someone who appeared to be limping then sent them through the rift. The deftness and delicacy of the maneuver surprised and impressed Gale. Beast got stopped with similar precision, but far less care.

Once a single person passed through the rift, the rest rushed through. More came from the buildings, screaming as Wendigo burst through the walls.

"I'm going after Wendigo. Got a good idea how to deal with it," Jade launched a chain at the shattered wall, pulling herself up once it attached.

"Split them up, I've got Basilisk," Volt commanded as she flew off, blasting the slimy Oghrodi back.

Quake flourished his bats and faced Golem. "Guess you're mine."

Doubt nagged at the back of Gale's mind. Maybe he really was unneeded. Before he could spiral, Quake spoke up.

"Gale, I hate to ask, but can you back all of us up? You've got the speed for it."

Quake wielded both bats easily and blocked Golem's swinging appendages. Even while speaking he could track the flailing limbs. Civilians were panicking as the deflected blows caused the ground to rumble. When Golem's arms spread out, Gale dashed forward and knocked one of its legs out from under it. The monster recovered, but now had much further to go if it was going to intercept the hostages.

"We need to hit hard and fast. If everyone gets out before us, Mizzek still wins," Gale explained quickly. "They'll let every prisoner escape if it means we're stuck here."

"I knew they wanted the Glaives," Quake scoffed. "Even if Mizzek had one, they couldn't be a superhero."

"Pray tell, what am I missing?" Mizzek taunted through the intercom.

Quake rushed towards Golem, blocking Gale from sight. "Everything."

It was the first time he'd gone on the offensive all fight. With a fierce swing, Quake aimed his left bat at Golem's head. Normally, he avoided a kill like that. There had to be a plan. Gale's mind raced for the best option. Stones clicked as Golem's right tentacle extended and solidified over its head to block the incoming attack. Without pulling back, Quake repeated his attack with the right bat. It was stopped even faster but caused Golem to leave its torso wide open.

The distance between them was too much for Quake to deliver a solid attack. The Oghrodi could easily reach him. One leg remained firmly on the ground as the other started whipping at the Glaive. Dents quickly appeared across its form from the fierce assault, yet Quake remained steady. Nothing would shake the hopeful superhero. His large back was a sight Gale was familiar with. Staring at it, an idea formed in his mind. Likely the same idea Quake had.

The guy's trust knew no bounds and Gale would make sure to deliver on expectations. He rushed forward, planted a foot on Quake's back, and leapt off. He activated his leg thrusters and soared. At the peak of his jump, the armor on his back split open over the shoulder blades to reveal two more thrusters. Those propelled him towards Golem's chest. Gale extended his leg and steadied his body. The impact forced the Glaive's boot into the cracked stone of the Oghrodi's torso. Gale released his leg with another kick and flipped away from the monster. Its stony face was unreadable, but it took a defensive stance. Golem was scared.

In the distance, Volt rapidly fired electric blasts at the massive flail blocking her line of sight. Basilisk slithered around a massive pool of slime.

Gale yelled. "Quake, you—"

"I've got this," he declared. "Help Volt."

Gale tore off towards their flying comrade without hesitation. His treads could keep up with Basilisk and Volt. Unfortunately, the gooey outer layer of the Oghrodi's body was probably more impact resistant than before. Volt should be able to burn through the liquid shield with a clear shot. An idea hatched in Gale's mind. It was reckless, but it would give his friend an opening.

He neared the battle, but Basilisk masterfully kept both Glaives away. Spikes rained in all directions as the tail tracked Volt. An equally effective offense and defense.

"Any ideas?" Volt asked.

"If I create an opening, can take out its armor?" Gale replied.

"Of course!"

Gale grunted affirmatively. "Keep it distracted."

While the others were unable to fight Basilisk in its pool of slime, Gale could. He had yet to find terrain his hooked treads couldn't grip. A volley of shots kept the flail airborne. Gale just had to worry about spikes. Volt flitted about even more erratically. She needed to keep the monster's focus until Gale made his move. Grunts of pain caught in the voice comms, but Volt didn't back down. Even as pieces of her armor cracked, she continued her assault.

Gale finally got within reach of the monster and planted a foot against it. Basilisk snickered at the seemingly ineffective attack, which allowed Gale the opportunity to ride his treads up the monster's ridiculously long tail. He wrapped his body around the base of the circular orb in hopes of reminding the monster of their previous encounter. With a mighty swing Basilisk brought the metallic ball to the ground. Gale loosened his grip just enough to reposition and land on his feet. Immense pain shocked his body, but the warrior refused to release his catch. Spikes jutted out of the tail into Gale's side, piercing through his armor and rib. Still, he refused to let go. Basilisk could attack all it wanted, but its tail could no longer reach Volt.

This was the best opening Gale could get her.

Light gathered in the flying Glaive's blasters until it fused into a single shining sun. A beam shot out, colliding with Basilisk's upper body. Its slime boiled into a bubbling pool of mucus. The viscosity was lost, shedding off the Oghrodi in clumps as it screamed in pain.

"How do we get these things out of here?" Volt asked.

Gale's brain was firing on all cylinders now. None of them were willing to cross the line with the monsters. They needed portals of their own to displace the Oghrodi.

"Think you can handle Basilisk for now? I've got an idea," Gale said.

"No doubt!" Volt replied.

Retreating from the flail was difficult with the pain in Gale's side. Thankfully, Basilisk was fully focused on the electrifying superhero that had melted its shield. With effort, Gale dove away then rushed the decrepit buildings. The flood of prisoners had slowed with only a few left near the rift. One caught his eye, gesturing wildly to a shaking building. The same one Jade chased Wendigo into.

Gale raced inside and found a stairwell with few functional steps left. Destination unclear, he took a slow ride up the walls and listened for sounds of struggle.

"Gale, down one floor!" Jade yelled. "Got civilians and can't fight Wendigo at the same time."

Instead of dropping to her level immediately, Gale entered the floor he was next to. To no surprise, the walls and ground had caved in from battle. They made perfect openings for a surprise attack. Gale skated along the wall of the corridor, slowly picking up speed. It had to be perfect so he didn't overshoot.

The moment he glimpsed Wendigo, Gale leapt through a hole and swung a fist at its back. Needles covered its spine, but Gale didn't hesitate. Some spikes shattered on impact while others stabbed back into the monster. Wendigo yelped in pain and skittered back.

Several layers of chains had become a powerful wall against the Oghrodi. They parted to reveal two young children gripping tightly onto Jade's legs.

"Gale, get these kids out of here!" she commanded. "I'll handle this thing."

"We need its beacon," Gale said.

"Why? Actually, nevermind. Least you're sharing the plan." Jade carefully released herself from the children and handed them to her friend. "Can you make the jump down?"

It was possible, but the impact might shake up the kids. Better that than dying here. Gale cradled them in his arms and leapt out of the nearest opening. He handed the kids over to the few remaining prisoners. The last civilian ran through the portal.

Gale turned his full attention to the Oghrodi, ready to fight.

"Get to the rif—" Quake's voice cut short.

He and Volt were nowhere to be seen. Only the crumpled form of Golem and Basilisk could be found. There was no progressive shrinkage of the rift as Gale had expected. One instant a massive portal covered part of the faux desert, the next it was gone.

The doors to the prison shut with a loud click and the constant alarm finally silenced.

When Gale turned back to where the rift once stood he was met by Mizzek. Golden metal protruded across their skin like a primitive suit of armor. The air of calm faded from the impostor as fury took over.

Stand Out Fit In

"I am willing to admit when I am wrong." Mizzek's voice was icy as they slowly marched towards Gale. "The other Glaives were stronger than I anticipated. If they had not been dealt with my comrades would be irreversibly wounded."

Gale frantically searched his periphery for any sign of his friends. All he found were the decrepit city and beaten Oghrodi. A quick vibration through his suit confirmed no one was hidden within the structures.

Taking a fighting stance, he asked, "What did you do to them?"

"I sent them back home," Mizzek answered.

They had operated the rift solo; it made sense the Glaives were sent away. Capturing them would be too risky, and this way, Gale was left alone.

"With more users you could have made the rifts go somewhere else," Gale said.

"You figured that out with one look?" Mizzek asked.

"I figured it out thanks to years of studying rift anomalies. All those pocketed disasters couldn't come from the same place. Not at the same time at least."

Mizzek scoffed. "It is disappointing how unremarkable you are with so much intelligence. You always require someone else to do the heavy lifting. Ray, Eve, Sarah, even me. But alone, you are worthless."

Ducking into range, Gale threw a right hook. The Oghrodi blocked, grabbing the warrior's forearm. Metal creaked and twisted as Mizzek tightened their grip. Several torturous seconds passed as the suit's arm was crushed, breaking the body within. Gale's mind reeled from the pain.

Mizzek shook their head. "See? Predic—"

Without breaking out of the grip, Gale jumped and sent his left leg at the monster's temple. He almost made contact. Unfortunately, Mizzek grabbed the limb out of the air. The pain of bones breaking was less noticeable this time. Probably because of adrenaline. Blood poured out of the torn suit as Gale was held aloft in Mizzek's grasp.

"Surprising. But not enough," the Oghrodi grumbled. "That you have such tenacity despite your obvious lack of faith in yourself is marvelous."

"What the hell are you talking about?" Gale spat.

Mizzek's grip didn't change, but sharp, spreading pain burned Gale's body. No amount of adrenaline could mask the agonizing sensation of skin peeling off in layers. Normally the armor unequipped in a flash, but now it disintegrated like ashes.

Agonizing screams escaped the masked warrior. It was incomparable to stabbed ribs or broken bones. Gale felt his entire being ripped away from him in a fiery blaze. As his clothing appeared, Gale remembered how vulnerable he really was. Finally, the helmet shattered to reveal the face behind it; my face.

Aside from the battle wounds, my skin was actually undamaged. The air still stung like fresh sunburn. Bones jutted out of my arm and leg, hidden only by my jeans. It was peculiar witnessing how the Glaive had replaced my clothes. No cuts in the slightest, but the fabric was tinted a deep red with blood.

"Oghrodi transform due to our convictions. It is why I was unsurprised by Ray, Eve, and Sarah's utilization of the Glaives," Mizzek explained. "Each has a firm belief, no matter how foolish, that drives them to fight. You, on the other hand, have doubted yourself the entirety of your life. This transformation is yours, yet I am able to peel it away. That would not have happened to any of the others. *That* is why you are still here. To prove to my brethren that even the weakest, most pathetic humans, pose a threat to us."

While Mizzek's insults cut, they weren't wrong. I followed my father's logic about a person's worth. I didn't believe in myself since I'd done nothing worth believing in. My best friend led Project Glaive and gave me a spot on a whim. Gale's capabilities were provided by the smartest person I knew. My confidence came from the wise words of the girl I loved. I never qualified for the job given to us. If not for Ray, Eve, and Sarah covering me, Operation Beacon would have failed too.

Before I could spiral further, a strange thought occurred to me: when my Glaive was ripped away, *I* hurt, not my body, my self. Doffing armor doesn't hurt like that. Ray's philosophy of "it's just a suit" was wrong. Hell, even my glasses had reappeared on my face. Just like the Oghrodi, my transformation was a part of me. Maybe I was a monster.

I imagined Ray laughing at that, taunting me for being so dramatic. I wasn't a monster. *I* held back the horrors attacking our planet. People didn't trust an unknown suit to save them. My friends didn't trust a faceless warrior to support them. Gale, my mask, inspired others; it wasn't meant to hide my spirit.

On instinct, I flung my good arm forward and jabbed Mizzek's eyes. They screamed and threw me across the virtual desert. Broken bones slid across cold metal. It was excruciating, but not anywhere near as bad as the previous burning pain. I slammed a fist against the ground to stop myself. Slowly, I pushed myself up onto my capable knee, ignoring every instinct to go limp.

I spit out a wad of blood. "You know, I feel a lot better now that I'm out of that suit. Gave me a lot of clarity. Thanks for that, Mizzek."

They growled, "Push yourself any further and you will die."

"Been doing that every day for seventeen years. Guess I should thank my parents."

"Parents who consider you a disappointment."

My mind flashed to the dreaded look on Dad's face when he realized what Mizzek was. "I'm realizing they can be wrong about people. Especially me."

Mizzek barked out a harsh laugh, one I'd heard from my father many times in my life. Honestly, it made me reel more than any of their other insults. It also reminded me that I was as disappointed of my father as he was of me. There was no reason I should be cowering from his insecure habits.

"Based on what you have shown me, your parents are pragmatic people." Mizzek's low voice carried across the gap as they approached. "You move through life blindly hoping others will show you the way."

I grimaced. "You're not wrong. I should've realized others have been showing me the way for a while." I pushed myself to stand straight so we were eye level with each other. "I never believed in myself, but I'm starting to. After all, a reckless plan I came up with on the fly ended up working. The prisoners are safe and most of the Glaives are gone."

"Yet, you remain."

"I'm not worried about that part. I may be new to believing in myself, but my faith in those three is unshakable. They'll get me out of here."

Mizzek closed in and my whole body continued to shake. But Mizzek wasn't rushing in lieu of chatting. Next time I saw Ray, I'd tell him about this monologue. The thought of my best friend reminded me of everything he'd try to convince me of. My heart pounded like mad, but not from pain. It was about time I committed to Ray's mindset. The mindset a young me aspired to.

I shifted my good leg back and raised my unbroken hand to the rim of my glasses.

"Un..."

I drew out the syllable, running my finger along the top edge of my Scabbard before extending my arm out. A crisp snap echoed from my fingers.

"-sheathe!"

The smirk on my face vanished behind my Glaive's mask. The second skin I'd failed to appreciate wrapped around me in a familiar embrace. Even broken limbs didn't hinder my joy as the suit reconstituted and HUD came online.

"Puppeteer."

The fiber-bound inner armor twisted and tightened, forcing my broken bones into normal angles. There was no way I could move them normally, but with this mode I didn't have to. Puppeteer ignored my body, allowing me to control the Glaive directly.

Would this mess me up permanently? Probably. But I would survive. Then I could thank Eve properly for installing such a ridiculous last minute codeword.

"Tell me, even if they could save you? What is your plan to stall?" Mizzek asked.

There was no "if" about it. According to my vibrations, there were only three Oghrodi in the room and I had sight on all of them. Wendigo was gone. Surely Jade had taken the monster with her during the forced retreat.

I beckoned Mizzek towards me with a finger while getting in a fighting stance and declared, "I'm gonna kick your ass."

Mizzek shook their head and stepped within inches of my reach. "That is the single stupidest thing that you have ever uttered. You are an insignificant speck within your own species. Your very progenitors view you as a failure. You face someone who has already defeated you as if you stand a chance. What are you to think such a thing?"

My first thought was that I was a failure of a son. But my friends knew I wasn't. Then I considered I might be a bad friend. Thinking those words invited the deserved wrath of the people who cared most for me. Weird that every idea I had of myself was dictated by my parents. Their need for me to be exactly what they wanted held me back from being who I needed to be. It was getting in the way of my own survival. Ray's confident voice echoed in my head and a manic smile sliced across my face.

"Simple." I stepped in with the motion Agent Daniels drilled into me. "I'm a fucking superhero."

My once broken arm shot forward with the support of my suit. It hurt to move, but for puppeteering to work I needed to remain focused. Adrenaline coursed through my body and I aimed through Mizzek's chest. Overconfident, the Oghrodi missed their chance to block and left the perfect opening. The strike sent them flying back across the desert. The gold metal across their body allowed them to slide smoothly before regaining footing. Mizzek looked up only to find me within reach again. Both their hands shot out to the side and tried to slam me between them. Metal spikes jutted out of the palms on a crash course with my skull.

I raised my arms to my temple and stepped in to block the monster's wrists. Instead of bouncing off, they put on the pressure. We stood in a stalemate.

They scoffed. "You rely too heavily on—"

I jumped and kicked out. Aiming was a struggle so instead of hitting Mizzek's chest I caught their right shoulder and hip. Enough force sent them back again. They cried out as the treads of my boots ripped through their skin.

"My fists!" I hoped Agent Daniels would never hear the next words out of my mouth, "A better mentor than you taught me that already."

We stepped toward each other, but halted when the entire room lurched to the side. Within seconds it righted and an emergency alarm blared. I caught the words "tear" and "backfire." Before I could figure anything out, the room turned again, this time part of the wall tore off. No hall appeared on the other side, only the inky depths of space surrounding a familiar blue marble. Portions of the gigantic metallic spaceship were engulfed in rifts that rapidly appeared and disappeared. Loose pieces floated for mere seconds before fresh portals swallowed them up.

"What did you do?!" Mizzek rushed in and landed a heavy strike on my head.

Rather than recoiling, I stayed in reach and focused on quick hits instead of hard impacts. "I told you they'd come for me. Did you think your ship would survive the retrieval effort?"

Though I could keep Mizzek from getting a solid attack in, blocks did little to minimize the pain. Of course, Agent Daniels was right. Fighting a monster with boxing was foolish. Size didn't matter when an errant swing could be lethal. My body screamed to stop, but my mind kept pushing. The retrieval plan I'd made had been improved to torment an armada by three lunatics I'd do anything for. That included fighting until I had nothing left.

I swept Mizzek's leg and knocked them off balance. Rather than regain footing, they forced a transformation. Massive golden wings burst from their back and carried them skyward.

"That's just not fair!" I yelled.

"I am tired of your stubborn resistance! I have more than enough proof for my commanders," Mizzek barked back.

"So you're just gonna fly away?"

In a flash, they were on me with gold claws extending from human hands. Blood gushed from the hip they skewered. Mizzek might have held me there, if a rift hadn't suddenly appeared above us. The gravitational pull was beyond anything I'd felt before and forced the blade out of my side.

Suddenly the portal vanished and I was back on my feet. Distant pieces of the ship began to vanish. Smaller rifts appeared nearby and stole away Basilisk and Golem. The false sky overhead tore away. All that remained was a ruined neighborhood occupied by the meanest bird I'd ever met.

Mizzek came down momentarily to grab then carry me towards the void above. The ship's artificial gravity held strong.

"This universe is kill or be killed. You should have been smart enough to take my advice the first time I offered it. You might not have ever ended up here."

The harsh edge of their voice did little to shake me. I headbutted their chin and forced them to bite their tongue. It wasn't a powerful attack, but it stunned even the strongest foe. I freed myself from their grasp.

"That's not what superheroes do," I insisted, releasing my grip and plummeting towards the remnants of the prison.

No amount of physical augments or shock absorption helped. My entire body screamed when I landed, begging for this to end. But I wouldn't fall. Even if I wasn't rescued, I wouldn't let Mizzek be the last one standing. Unfortunately, no amount of visualization made my legs move. I ran only on fumes. My familiar fighting stance was manageable.

Mizzek calmly descended and mimicked it. Even if my legs didn't work, my arms still had power. Mizzek flexed their fists, wrapping them in golden metal.

"This is what humans do, no?" They smirked. "Fine. I will kill you as a human would."

They threw a hurricane of punches faster than anything I'd ever experienced. Every instinct ran on overdrive to match the rapid attacks. Our fists pounded against each other repeatedly. I faded in and out of consciousness, but I never let up. I didn't have Mizzek's alien endurance. There was no logical way I'd last longer than them. Metal shredded under the alien's golden knuckles and fluttered around us like confetti. My armor slowly tore down to the flesh underneath. The motions were so familiar. There were no thoughts as I endlessly swung my fists. My eyes constantly sought an opening in the dizzying frenzy.

Finally, I caught a misstep. A small rift appeared, forcing Mizzek a half step back, and their entire defense fell apart. It was only a second, maybe less. I pulled myself into as perfect a form as I could manage. Before Mizzek could recover, I threw out the only punch Agent Daniels willingly taught me. This one stronger than anything I could manage before I accepted that Gale and I were one in the same.

"Overdrive."

My body twisted fiercely, forcing the weight of my fist to fling my arm out. Using the thrusters across my entire suit, I blasted forward. If not for the Glaive, my shoulders would've ripped out of their sockets. Mizzek's sternum breaking felt unlike anything I'd ever experienced. They cried in surprise and pain as they keeled over. I pushed with all my might and forced them through the rift before it closed.

My legs gave out and I fell to the ground, spent. My HUD indicated no more Oghrodi. I rolled onto my back and stared at the exploding wreckage floating in space.

I thought of my amazing friends, without whom I couldn't have beaten Mizzek. When believing in myself wasn't enough, they had made my goal attainable.

I raised my bloody fist and screamed at the top of my lungs. "I want to go home!"

I thought they might actually hear me. They always had, even when I didn't know I needed them. When a rift appeared over me, far less powerful than the last, no part of me was surprised. A red armored hand reached out and clasped around mine. Then a yellow one grabbed my forearm before several green chains wrapped the rest of my body. Together, they pulled me through.

Home

A cool wind awoke me from slumber. I'd only ever seen this room on tour, a private one in a GPA infirmary. An end table separated me from another empty sickbed. My glasses and phone sat on top. Thanks to the thick casts covering my left leg and right arm, it was hard to move. Portions of my flesh were stitched and bandaged. Gauze covered parts of my face that had scraped across the Oghrodi prison floor.

I rose slowly, donning my glasses then checking my phone. Three things caught my immediate attention. The weather app stated we were in Madison, not Nebraska. Likely, I'd been moved during the four days I was apparently unconscious. Neither worried me as much as the 26 missed calls from Mom. Even more surprising was one from my father. Appeasing them was crucial, but that didn't mean I had to call Dad.

Mom picked up on the second ring. "Anand, are you awake?! Hold on, we're coming, *beta*."

"No!" I said without thinking. I had no idea how much they knew, but it made sense my injuries weren't hidden.

"What do you mean 'no'? I knew this was a bad idea. You got hurt because that Agent Daniels couldn't protect you. How could they let monsters attack children? I won't—"

"Enough, Mom! No one 'let' monsters attack us. Agent Daniels did everything he could to protect all of us. I'll be up to snuff in no time. I'm resilient." I took a deep breath. "I have to debrief here and then I'll come home. How are y— You're stressed. How's Dad doing?"

There was a long pause as Mom calmed herself down on the other end of the line. "Dad is doing well. He rested for a full day when he got back."

Anand scoffed. "That's more than he's rested his entire life."

Mom stifled a laugh. "Don't tell him you said that. He's coming to talk with you."

"Oh. Okay."

"Anand? How are you? Why haven't you called?" That was Dad. Always business.

"Good, just woke up," I replied dryly. "Sorry."

"Hm. That's fine. I didn't see you at the base," Dad said. "Nebraska is desolate. They flew us back in luxury. It was the least they could do for failing to protect us."

"Yeah."

"Mom is wondering when you will come home. You shouldn't just stay at the office."

It was a wild thing for someone who lived for work to say. Not to mention, he had to know I was bedridden with broken bones. It wouldn't surprise me if I needed to stay around for observation.

"There's a few things I need to finish up here," I answered. "I'll see what the director says but I think I'll be home soon."

I heard rapid footsteps approaching from the hall, but figured something happened on the base that wasn't my business.

"Right. Good." Dad trailed off. "Can you also do me a favor while you're there?"

I couldn't stop myself from scoffing. "I never thought you'd ask me for a favor. What do you need?"

"I assume Gale works from your base. Thank him for me."

"Yeah, can do." The door to my room opened. "Anything else?"

Ray, Eve, and Sarah burst inside, clambering over each other. Agent Daniels and Director Graves followed behind with their usual decorum. Everyone noticed the phone and paused. Dad cleared his throat and I tried to focus on him.

I strained to hear the words my father dared not utter. Apparently, he was proud of me. The longer he searched for more words, the less I cared. To his knowledge, I had almost died. Yet here he was, failing to comfort his own son or give him a semblance of acceptance.

I cut him off. "Okay. See ya later." Then hung up.

The moment the phone was down, my friends wrapped me in a tight hug. It was the most satisfying feeling I'd ever felt, minus the pain in my arm. The others noticed my grimace.

"Shit, sorry buddy," Ray said as he quickly released me. He grabbed a chair to my right. "Good to have you back."

"Good to be back."

Eve patted my shoulder and took the seat next to Ray. "I figure you're good to debrief. That's why we brought them along."

Sarah remained silent, grabbing the only seat next to my good arm. She rested hers, wrapped lightly in bandages, atop it.

Director Graves stepped in. "How are you feeling, Anand?"

"Better," I replied. "Honestly, way better than I expected."

"Yes, we should discuss that. Your body heals incredibly fast. We're still conducting tests to figure out the cause. You'll need to stay here a few more days until we get concrete results."

I didn't mind one bit. In fact, I was thankful for extra time to figure out how to deal with my parents. I would at least have them visit but luckily that limited my time with them.

"Sorry for all the trouble I caused," I said. "How'd you guys get me out anyway? That ship was wrecked."

Director Graves opened the floor for my friends to explain. When they had arrived, Sarah locked Wendigo down until the first agent on the scene, Agent Daniels, killed it. Lab techs rifled through the Oghrodi in search of its beacon. It was taken to the very room we failed to defend. In the commotion, we hadn't realized only the containment structure was damaged. The rest of the pillar still functioned.

Sarah replicated the spherical covering with her chains and held the beacon in place while rifts tore up the Oghrodi ship.

To facilitate all the Glaives working in the same place, Director Graves permitted use of a special tablet that could interface with any GPA device. Eve handled modifying rift values for size and strength while Ray input the coordinates. In minutes, they understood the workings of the portals which allowed them to assist directly.

"I'm just glad Gale's tracker never failed," Eve said. "Once you interfaced with the ship, we always knew your location."

"It feels weird that Mizzek ended up helping us even if they didn't realize it," Ray added.

Director Graves cleared her throat. "While I understand keeping Mizzek a secret, we will discuss their revelations at a later time. For now, appreciate the change you have wrought."

"Are the Oghrodi gone?" I asked.

"For now." Agent Daniels interjected.

"It would be poor form to expect them to leave us in peace," Director Graves explained. "Your team acted ingeniously to not only save you, but also steal data from the Oghrodi. Portions of the ship were sent off to different GPA bases across the world. Meanwhile, every Oghrodi we found was sent off to different corners of space."

"What if they end up on other alien planets?" I asked.

Sarah looked at me then pointed at Ray. "I told you so."

"I'm sorry!" Ray threw his hands up in surrender. "We only found the few we fought anyway. That ship was mostly empty."

"Mizzek tricked us," Eve said. "Ever since the Runner was stolen we were playing their game."

"Regardless, you've changed our planet's fate," Director Graves explained. "Hope shines in the eyes of humanity once again. We have gained new tools to prepare for their return. This time they won't be attacking a defenseless planet. That wouldn't have been possible without each and every one of you."

Finally, people felt safe. However, this wasn't the end. I glanced between my friends and let out a long sigh of relief. Whatever came next, we would face it together.

"I think the GPA should properly honor the Glaives. The superheroes, not the suits," I suggested. "Show that they're still around to watch over humanity."

"That implies you would be able to unsheathe without the presence of a rift," Director Graves countered.

"Check the cahlium levels. With how many rifts just ripped up our atmosphere I have a hunch we can transform whenever we need to," I said. "To protect people."

Director Graves considered for a moment then slowly nodded. "I will see what we can do. In the meantime, rest up. We can discuss your potential permanent positions with the GPA at a later time."

Ray piped up, "Do we get paid?"

This was met with a jab to the ribs from Eve.

The boy rubbed his side. "It's a valid question."

Director Graves left, but Agent Daniels lingered.

"If we're hiring you, I'll make sure you're paid," he affirmed, then turned to me. "Looks like you figured out how to kick. Try not to break your leg next time."

"Would it kill you to just say 'good job' like a normal person?" Sarah complained. "I mean you've been worried sick about him."

Agent Daniels didn't so much as flinch. The man's professional demeanor was inspiring. Maybe I'd have him teach me that next. Then again, my friends understood me because of obvious and outward feelings. The stoic man and I stared at each other. He never stuck around for long chats. It would be a while until I could train again. Pestering him just wasn't possible day-to-day. I chose my next words carefully.

"I ended the fight with a single punch," I said. "I mean, I punched a lot, but the last one was—"

"Solid." A smile appeared on Agent Daniels' face before he turned away. While leaving, he threw out one last, "Good job, kid."

The presence of the agents was like teachers. Nice, but hard to cut loose around.

My friends began filling me in on classes I missed. Homework piled up and finals were already fast approaching. Surprising myself, I found I wasn't stressed about it. I knew I could clear those hurdles. Maybe not perfectly, but I'd stick the landing.

"Can we get brunch?" I asked.

"For sure!" Ray replied.

"Mind waiting outside while I change?"

When Sarah released my hand to step outside, I felt its absence. That weight was one I could get used to.

Once everyone left, I slowly changed, then struggled with how to stand. Eventually, I called them back in for help. My body was too damaged for crutches and we couldn't find a wheelchair with a controller. A manual one would have to do.

Without asking, Ray was at the back, guiding us through the hallway. Eve stood beside me, discussing the new things she wanted to test. Sarah chimed in intermittently with her ideas. I was too distracted by the bandages covering her hand to respond. Clearly handling Wendigo and fulfilling my request for a beacon did a number on her. Ray noticed me staring and jerked the wheelchair forward, causing my hand to bump Sarah's.

"What's up?" she asked.

I heard more than saw Ray and Eve's snickers. Sarah's soft smile pulled my full attention. My impulsiveness had saved my life and I'd embraced it because of her. Leaning on it again didn't feel like a bad idea.

"I know your hand is hurt, but do you think you can push my wheelchair on our date?"

Her eyes went wide, a familiar blush blooming across her cheeks. Eve rushed to Sarah's side and whispered something while Ray planted a firm hand on my shoulder in support. Even now, they schemed and laughed freely. My own face burned from embarrassment but I couldn't help smiling. For the first time in a long while, I felt like a normal teenager.

Epilogue

Jillian Graves sat in her office, watching over the hangar of the Madison GPA base. Vehicles had been removed to make room for a massive chunk of the Oghrodi spaceship. For it to have monitored Earth for nearly a quarter of a century was illogical. But the world had been getting further from any semblance of logic for a long time. This machine had likely contained an unfathomably potent source of power yet some children's' scheme had destroyed it.

A deep sigh escaped Jillian's soul as she wheeled her desk chair back to its place. The lab techs could worry about the Oghrodi research and report back. She needed to focus on the aftermath of the retrieval operation. It was a stroke of genius by Anand to request the retrieval of a beacon. The fact Sarah brought a live Oghrodi back to ensure an intact organ was beyond impressive. Once it was active, Eve and Ray took charge in making and executing a plan to rip apart a massive ship. It was brilliant work yet Jillian couldn't bring herself to bask in the victory.

Something went wrong with the rapid rift creation and pieces of the ship were missing. GPA agents were scouring the planet in search of them. A public announcement had to be made for everyone's safety. Unfortunately, humanity had its own bad actors. If a couple kids were able to figure out how to create magical armor, there was no telling what others could do. It was a blessing that the young Glaives had good intentions. They truly were superheroes; as silly as that title felt.

Two knocks rapped against her door. Jillian knew who it was. Alec Daniels stepped into the office before shutting the entrance behind him.

"I heard you got the results," he said while slumping into the chair opposite Jillian.

For some reason, he lost all professionalism in one-on-one situations. Thankfully, he had the good sense not to act this way in settings where people might challenge either's authority.

"Yes, it is as you expected." Jillian pressed her thumb against the scanner on one of the drawers next to her. Once it was open, she retrieved a folio with four packets inside and handed it to her subordinate. He flipped through each of them quickly, knowing exactly what he was looking for.

"God dammit, this is insane! Cahlium levels in the atmosphere might rise, but humans have remained steady all this time. Have we tested anyone else?" he asked.

"How do you suggest we do that?" Jillian inquired. "Younger candidates would provide better data, but the GPA cannot demand the bloodwork of anyone not involved in our organization."

"What about the prisoners from the ship?"

"Only the children present had cahlium in their blood and it was at normal levels."

The words garnered a grim look from Alec. It took little for him to lose the uncaring facade when it came to his wards. While he'd offered to teach the young Glaives, it was clearly in hopes of scaring them off. Keeping his distance had become difficult as they withstood his grueling training. The man had grown a soft spot in that impenetrable shell of his.

"What if we tested other people with tainted blood?" he asked.

Jillian shook her head, "They're all dead, Alec. Oghrodi blood transmission only happens on battlefields. Even with the Glaives' help we lost over a dozen agents. There's no telling if the integration of alien blood did anything to them."

Alec kneaded his head in one hand while riffling the papers with the other. "The Oghrodi blood and cahlium must be reacting with each other. Literally all the kids' cuts healed in a day! Anand will be out of those casts in a fraction of the time it takes the average person."

"You're correct. Even his deeper cuts are almost gone. Though they will leave scars."

There was a tense silence when Jillian stopped speaking. The man intently awaited her next suggestion. Both of them knew what had to happen. Too many oddities existed relating to the Glaives. Intrusive tests needed to be conducted, but that wasn't part of the deal when they joined the GPA.

"We've got samples from Wendigo, right?" Alec asked. "Oghrodi blood already has cahlium in it. We can see if it'll modify my levels after an infusion."

"We can't know if the effect it has on you will be the same as the mutated generation." Jillian paused then nodded slowly. "But I cannot deny the appeal of such an offer. Thank you. It will be one less headache."

Alec took his eyes off the paper in his hands and looked at the tired director. She'd been going full force since Operation Beacon failed. In all the years they'd known each other, she'd never shown this much unease.

"What's on your mind, Jill?" Alec asked.

Jillian let out a deep sigh. "The lost pieces of the Oghrodi ship. Citizens might be aiding in the search but I doubt we've gotten reports about every sighting. Alien technology is bound to garner unwanted attention."

"You're worried about another Glaive."

"Created by someone lacking the morality of a superhero fanboy." Jillian smiled weakly. "I'm unable to tell which is worse between that and the advancing mutation."

"We really need to get on equal footing with the Glaives." Alec rose from his seat, tucked the folder under his arm and turned to leave. "I'll let you get some rest. Let me know when we start the transfusions."

There was always a little madness in his eyes, but Jillian learned long ago that was present in all her best agents. It was disquieting that it manifested in the young recruits as well. Who knew if it would worsen with their evolving physiques. Jillian quieted those concerns, trusting in her newest recruits. They weren't ordinary agents. The world now had real, identifiable beacons of hope in the form of four heroic teenagers.

About the author

Bhav Das-Romain is a non-binary Indian obsessed with heroes of all kinds. Escaping to fantastical worlds saved by hopeful individuals was their favorite childhood pastime. To this day they collect action figures of their favorite characters from comics and videogames. They live in Madison, WI with their wonderful spouse. Coffee and chai flow through their veins. If they could be anything else, it'd be a superhero.